I Choose

With whom does your heart lie?
by JLorain

Copyright © 2020 JLorain

Scripture quotations, unless otherwise indicated,are from The New King James, The Passion Translation, The New Living Translation of the Bible.

ISBN 978-0-615-77090-1
ISBN (Digital)

For permission requests, solicit the writer via the address below:

JLorain
Mailing Address: PO Box 7664
Columbus, OH 43207
Email Address: jlorainco@gmail.com

TABLE OF CONTENTS

DEDICATION

This book was inspired by my babies Lexii and Raaya. We have experienced so much together. In the spiritual and in the natural, God has covered, healed, taught, and blessed us. Never forget the power of the Holy Ghost and the power of prayer, for these have helped us withstand every test.

I love you . . .

THANK YOU

Thank you all for loving me. Your prayers have made me stronger. Your wisdom has helped me. Your support has encouraged me. Thank you for putting up with all my phone calls, answering all my questions. I love you guy's way more than all the words in the book.

Marvella Cummings, David Cummings, Apostle Mary Crutcher, DeTriece McCarrel & Lisa Steadman.

Thank you to everyone who has prayed for me and wished me well. Love you all!

FOREWORD

This book is well written. The flow, and balance of the word along with the practical applications are easy to receive and put into practice.

JLorain's thorough presentation of each character, their individual dilemma, how they interconnect with one another,and their personal outcomes mirrors what many people that you and I know are facing right now in 2020.

I quickly fell in love with Kim, Tim, Leah, Mrs. Karns, Tonya, Paul, and the other characters— they reminded me of several people that I know and even situations that I have experienced.

I Choose, literally brings front and center how our choices and decisions affect not only our personal life but the lives, relationships, and outcomes of those around us.

Every scripture utilized points to a way of escape out of every bad situation, circumstance, bad relationship, and/or bad habit. It all comes down to YOU utilizing the power of choice with that power being Jesus Christ.

CHOOSE wisely...

Apostle Voyd Bailey-Burks
Kingdom Covenant Intl. Church
Columbus, Ohio

LETTER FROM JLORAIN

I pray you and your family are healthy and blessed. I want to start off by saying thank you so much for purchasing my book. I appreciate you and pray blessings over your life. Writing the Second Edition of I Choose was exciting, rewarding, and refreshing.

I want to take a moment to share with you how I Choose was birthed. In 2006 I began writing a script for what was only to be a twenty-minute skit for the youth in the church I attended at the time. Well, God had other plans. It turned out to be a full production, which completely blew my mind. I had absolutely no idea how to be a stage director or even run a rehearsal. With the assistance of a very dear friend, Lisa Steadman, to whom I am so thankful for; it was a successful stage play. Again, God had other plans.

In 2010 I began transforming the manuscript for the First Edition of I Choose. Yet again, completely clueless how to write a manuscript, as it was my first publication. It was published for the first time in 2013. I Choose was written from a reflection of some of the things that has happened in mylife, feelings I have had, and things I have seen in the spirit. Those things have had a direct and indirect effect on my life—some good, and some bad. God has shown me through the years, many things, and the lessons learned are indescribable. Sharing those things with you is of importance to me.

Do you know who you are? It tookyears for me to be able to answer thatquestion, well into my adult life. Do you know whose you are? I have learned, you cannot love anyone unless you know who they truly are. What I mean by that is, you cannot love yourself unless you know who you are. Did you know you have value? You are valuable to God. So much so, you are worth everything to Him. Did you know that? Did you know that God loves you? Know your value, your purpose, and make your move. Jesus has already made His move, for you. He put the ball in your court after the cross.

Know this, every single thing you do, in your life, has a direct or indirect effect on you as well. Never get it twisted to think that there are no consequences to your actions, and in each situation, there is a message. Take the time to stop, pay attention, and listen to the message. Noone thing, no one person that is in your life,and no reaction from that one trial takes God by surprise. Let us keep it real guys, God is the real deal, and He loves us. He watches over us, and His Grace and mercyis everlasting.

Enjoy . . .

CHAPTER ONE

Five days before graduation, Kim is ready to say goodbye to her high school years yet afraid to say hello to change. The pressure that came from writing her future, choosing to say no to sex, drugs, and alcohol, along with carrying the issues of her friends, began to weigh heavily on her. Mentally and emotionally weak, Kim walked through the parking lot with her head hung low. With each step she took, feelings of depression, unhappiness, and loneliness grew.

After sitting down in front of a tree, Kim leaned back to take advantage of her solitude and write in her journal before the bell rang. Forever needing to pour out everything inside—her expression of life, her view of the things around her, and to allow her heart to speak; she began to write. Swallowing the lump in her throat,she held back the tears. This was the only thing she could do to find some sort of comfort.

"I'm hurting, Lord. I don't like it, and I don't know how to deal with it. I can't decide what degree I want to pursue. I don't want to worry about how I'm going to make it after high school, I and why my friend doesn't want to be friends. I'm lonely and it's really messed up."

"I don't consider myself the *baddest chick*, but dang, why am I still single? I can't dissect every area of my life and pinpoint the root cause of my issues, but *You* can. I don't know how to explain everything I'm feeling inside, so trying to get me to explain why is extremely out of the question."

Kim continued to write, even though her hands were shaking like a house during a storm. "I'm terrified because of the choices I made before giving my life to You, and the belief that I can make it, seems so far away. I hate what I see when I look in the mirror, and I just don't know what to do about it. Lord, I need help. It has taken a very long time for me to think of my interests, my needs, and my wants oversomeone else's. I've been suffering invisibly, until now. But no matter what, I have to get it together."

Kim had to keep her focus on nothing else but herself and God and trying to find the answers she desperately desired. One by one, students began to empty the buses. One of those students was Paul—a real, very outspoken, and extremely raw Christian. At first glance, one would say he was a thug or hood rat. However, he isnothing of the kind. Paul sees himself as God's little buddy. He makes it known that he has all the answers, or so he believes.He is a cool, laid-back Christian and a very good friend of Kim's.

Paul noticed her sitting off to the side, alone. What to do never entered his mind because Paul is firm on one thing. He is and forever will be connected to the Lord. This in turn, afforded him the right to tap in, whenever needed. He walked over, as if to just say hello, hoping she would open upand tell him about what was going on. As open as Kim is to the idea of helping someone else, she never allows others to dothe same.

Paul thought to himself, *Okay, this will never do*. Not knowing how she would respond, he took a deep breath and approached her. "Wassup, shorty?" He said with much hesitation.

Kim tried to hurry and wipe the tears from her face. "Hey Paul," she said. "Why do you keep calling me that? What are you trying to say?" Kim asked with much curiosity. At the same time trying her best to seem as though she had it all together.

Paul, being the friend that he is, knew something was going on with Kim. "What are you doing way down here by yourself? Is everything all right with you? Who do I need to have a discussion with? In the Christian way that I do, of course," he said jokingly. "Come on, Kim. I'm not gonna let you just not say anything. We go through this all the time. You're gonna open up to me today. Prepare your mind or do whatever it is you need to do to make that happen."

With puffy, blood-red eyes, Kim looked up and said, "You are crazy, Paul. I'm not really doing anything, just writing in my journal, trying to collect my thoughts, that's all. I'm going through some stuff, and I need to get it out. Nothing serious. What's good with you?" Kim asked. "And what's up with your attire today?"

"Nothing much with me, but it's early yet," Paul said. "Why you always smashin' my clothes, man?" Paul stepped back and gave Kim a dirty look.

Not sure how to take Paul's reaction, Kim said, "I'm not smashin' them, Paul. But as always, you look like you're trying to make a statement, and I'm not saying you don't look good doing it. You look good blendin' in."

"Yes, I'm always making a statement," Paul said as he laughed and pointed to the sky. "Ok, lay it on me because you know I have all the answers," Paul said with a serious look on his face.

"You really believe that, too. That's why it's so funny," Kim said. "Nah, I'm just glad everything you do, you do it for the one, the only one, who can make everything all right. Solid on what you believe and unwavering. I believe in your ministry, Paul, and I know you are pleasing God."

Paul stood there for a moment, nodding, agreeing with Kim. Being about his Father's business is what Paul strives for. After a long period of silence, Paul said, "Really though, Kim, you need answers from who and for what? Come on! Why you leaving me in the dark like this? I know it's deeper than you're making it out to be, writing down thoughts and stuff. Quit trippin'!"

"I need answers from God, Paul. I know you mean well, but only He can answer them. Things are getting a little out of control right now, and I don't know what to do. It doesn't help that people look at you like your issues are not important or serious enough to worry about, but they are to me. Not you, but other people do. Just because you're a Christian and a teenager, doesn't mean you don't have problems. It doesn't mean you ain't going throughanything. I don't like to tell people for fear of being judged or looked at like I'm trippin'for nothin'. I know you're not like that, but a lot of other people are."

Kim is a strong Christian teenager. It is not like her to show her deepest self, not even to her friends. It is amazing when you have an individual who is strong, yet sensitive, humble, but bold in her delivery. Kim is all those things, and her friends know it. She carries herself very well and seldom cracks under pressure. She comes from a single-parent household.

Kim is the older of two girls, and while her strength comes from God, she also gets a great deal from her mother.

Paul replies in all sincerity, "That's partly what a true friend is, Kim, and I try my best to be that for you. I hope I've never been one to judge you. But, you are not gonna sit here and act like you're not gonna tell me what the heck is going on. So, spill it."

"No, I don't want to go into it right now. I'm not even sure it would do any good at this point. I'm tired of crying about it," Kim said.

Paul, being the jokester that he is, said, "Well, you don't have to cry while you tell me."

"I don't know, maybe it's just me overreacting," she said softly. "But thank you. I'm sure I'll take you up on that offer one day," Kim said softly.

"Okay fine. I'll leave you to your searching then. I need you to holla at me later though." Paul's tone of voice was more than him speaking from the heart of a friend. It was from a place where only the spirit of God dwells. "Kim, okay?"

"I will. I promise, Minister Paul," she said with a sarcastic tone.

"Hey, Kim, ain't that your girl Tonya down there, looking straight up to no good? Real talk Kim. What is she doing?" Paul said with much displeasure, and with a tone that even Kim found disturbing.

Quickly, Kim dropped her books and stood to see what Paul was talking about. "Where? I don't see her. That can't be her anyway. She told me she wasn't coming today," Kim said.

"Okay, you can't see too good?" Paul said as he turned Kim's head in Tonya's direction. "Can you see her now?" As he pointed down to the end of the building, feelings of anxiety and disappointment came over him. "Wow, this is straight up crazy. What is she trying to do, prove a point?"

Kim, not wanting to believe what she saw, replied, "That's her? Can you tell what she's doing? Wait a minute, why are you buggin' out anyway? You've only known her for about a minute."

"Man, that was low, Kim, even for you. Nope, I can't tell what she's doing. But whatever it is, it can't be good. You know how Tim and Leah are. They ain't cool people, and she's hangin' with them!" Paul said with a concerned voice. "Tonya is a new Christian. Check it, and she was supposed to be my shorty. I can't chill with a girl like that."

"Hey, can you watch my stuff for me?" Kim began to walk down toward Tonya, to blast her out, but the look on Paul's face certainly showed that he did not agree.

Paul was speechless as he stood staring at Kim.

Not understanding why, Kim asked, "What, Paul?" As she threw her hands up. "I have to go down there. I'm not gonna just watch my girl be eaten by wolves and not do anything about it. What kind of friend would I be? Better yet, what kind of Christian would I be? That's a dark situation, and I choose to be a light and hopefully it can help them, too."

"The only thing you will do is cause problems. Why? Why are you goin' down there, Kim? Tell me that. If you go, what do you think she's gonna do? You're goin' there to let her have it, aren't you? And what would that solve? I think you should . . .um . . . not do that. Look at who she's hangin' with, Kim. Do you really want to get involved with people like them? I deal with kids like this all the time.

You've seen some of the teens at the church—the types of attitudes they have, the way they carry themselves, and the things they do in the streets. Trust me, she will not appreciate it if you go down there and front on her. You need to stop and think before you do it. If nothing else, knowthe first thing you're goin' to say."

"I'm not going to front on her, Paul, if that's what you want to call it. They are the reason why I want to go down there. I'm tired of having to explain why I do what I do. I just want to help her, in any way that I can. Why is that so wrong?"

Not understanding why. Kim refused to see where he was coming from. Paul leaned against the tree and put his head down as though he wanted to give up.

"*I know* your intentions, but will she? I never said you shouldn't do something. You have to pick the right time and place to do it though, Kim," he said with a serious expression. "There is nothing wrong with wanting to help her, and yes, you need to be ready in season and out," Paul said. "But you have to have the wisdom to know when to chill. Come on, man, do you want to lose her as a friend? Don't get in the way of what God may be trying to do.

If you want to reach her, you shouldn't do it that way. I mean, really, what are you going to say once you do get down there? Besides, what were we just talking about? You need to help yourself first. You are not in a good emotional place right now. When I walked up, your eyes were all red from crying. I mean, really, Kim, you were just crying a minute ago about your own issues. I just don't think you are in the position to try to talk or reason with Tonya at this moment."

"What I want to know is," Kim stressed, "when she started hanging with them two? This whole situation she's got goin' on is mind-blowing. What are you trying to say anyway? I'm not able to help someone else because I have issues?"

"What I'm saying, Kim, is there is a big difference between being influenced and being an influence. By going down there, you're being influenced by the devil because of your dislike for Leah and Tim. The devil doesn't want you to be a positive influence in Tonya's life, in any way, shape, or form. You know he will try whatever he can to break that friendship. Your friendship with Tonya is supposed to bring light in a very dark place.

Tonya is a new Christian, Kim. I don't believe she's quite out of the darkness yet. Being that positive influence, speaking into her life, introducing God to her, is the light that she needs. You don't think the devil knows that?" He asked. "It is not going down there and embarrassing her in front of them. You do not want her to feel attacked, Kim."

"Fine, I'm not going," Kim yelled. "I understand. I'll wait."

"Don't you get it? You sound as though you don't really understand where I am coming from. I can't even believe we are having this discussion. If we surround ourselves with people who are not good for us. We tend to walk like them and talk like them, not like Christ. We become blinded to the fact that we are striving to be like the Lord. At the same time, not realizing that being in the presence of evil, negative things, and toxic people and situations can have a negative effect on us. It's not that you don't love them, or you dislike them. You always want the best for people. However, you can love, respect, and pray from a distance, some you can let go. Others close enough to keep them in view, yet far enough not to feel the aftershock.

Tonya doesn't realize this yet, or maybe, she does and doesn't care. I mean, if you want to be real about it, maybe you shouldn't be hangin' with her."

"Slap your face for that," Kim said in response to the ridiculous statement from Paul. "I'm not going to stop hangin' with her. Why would I do that? Don't get me wrong, I understand what you are trying to say, but I've been there, done that, and I don't plan to go back to living that type of life. I'm good. I'm not saying I can't be tempted, but I am saying that we are friends for a reason, and I choose to allow God to use me in her life. She is a new Christian, Paul. I choose to be a light and that," she pointed, "is a dark situation."

Kim once again blew off what she's dealing with within herself, and Paul knew that. "Let me remind you that you are fragile right now. Chill out with responding off of your own emotion. Why do you continue to think someone else's issues are more important than yours? Cut it out, for real. Everyone is different, and so is their pain."

CHAPTER SUMMARY

Never question if your struggles matter to God, nor think they have no merit compared to someone else's. Most assuredly, never weigh your trials against someone else's. No one problem has the same effect on every individual, and it is important to not dismiss your feelings. Many times, we run to talk to a friend, wanting them to be a listening ear, and not necessarily wanting them to try and fix the issue, but oftentimes, God has another plan. Consider this scripture:

"So this is my command: Love each other deeply, as much as I have loved you. For the greatest love of all is a love that sacrifices all. And this great love is demonstrated when a person sacrifices his life for his friends."

John 15:12-13 TPT

I believe that when you are at your worst and at your best, a friend loves you. No matter what the situation, a true friend will be there to listen, to give advice, and to help, not cause pain or confusion. God places people in our lives for a number of reasons, whether to learn from, to lean on, and to have someone there when life is completely chaotic.

I am reminded of a tornado. Picture it— outside of the tornado, it is completely off the hook, to make it plain. However, in the center or eye of the tornado, it is probably almost calm. God wants to be that type of friend. When life gets too hard for you to handle alone, when you feel as though you cannot live anymore, and you want to give up, call on the one true friend, who will never leave you nor forsake you. Know that He is that calm you need in the midst of the storm. God will also put someone in place, who can bring about a type of calm during a storm or chaos. He places people in our lives for several reasons. I know you have that someone, that one person who can get you all the way together, if you will. That one person that will cry with you, laugh with you, and pray with you, as well. Sometime, all at the same time. If you do not, you better get you one.

Kim's emotions were all over the place because of her lack of faith. There was no way Kim was able to carry the problems of Tonya, as well as her own. We must come to a place in our lives when we have the wisdom to know it's time to be still. We cannot remain complacent where we are, and we cannot afford to move forward the way we are. We cannot continue to react out of our hurt, in order to be a light to someone. Paul's concern for Kim was warranted, and he realized Kim was not handling it very well. He realized Kim really did not want to talk about what was truly bothering her, and he chose not to push, this is another characteristic of a true friend that is very vital to the growth of a relationship or friendship.

Leah and Tim were students at the same high school and do not have the best reputations, in or out of school. Everyone tries to separate themselves from them—everyone, except Tonya. Paul was one who did not feel as though hanging with Leah and Tim would be a good decision. Now that Tonya has contact with them, Paul believes she could be influenced by their actions.

When you think about wisdom, do you think it can only come from someone older than you? Can it come from someone who has knowledge in a particular area, someone who has studied a certain craft, or someone who has gotten their knowledge from God? There are those who can recognize when they are in the presence of wisdom and others who cannot. Kim had to face, she felt responsible for Tonya as well.

You may know someone who is on a path of destruction, or a path you may feel is not correct. It is natural to want to turn them in the direction you think they should go. As a Believer, you must come to the understanding that some things are not for us to resolve. You are simply to be used by God, to be an example. Another scripture to consider:

"We can all draw close to him with the veil removed from our faces. And with no veil we all become like mirrors who brightly reflect the glory of the Lord Jesus. We are being transfigured into his very image as we move from one brighter level of glory to another. And this glorious transfiguration comes from the Lord, who is the Spirit."

2 Corinthians 3:18 TPT

This is to be our focus as Believers. Our walk, our lifestyle alone should minister and speak to someone else. How you are viewed as children of the Most High God can sometimes be the deciding factor for someone else in whether they want to know God. Kim had to choose if she was going to allow her emotions to lead her or let God lead her. The choice she makes will be the deciding factor of how her friendship with Tonya will end up. You must always try to choose the right thing to do. Making that choice on our own can be ridiculously hard. Allowing God to be your guide is the best thing you can do.

CHAPTER TWO

Questions, questions, questions. What rules do we follow or live by? There are many things, people, and influences that are screaming for our attention, telling us what to say and what not to say, and how to live our lives. I want to introduce three types of people. Type Number One knows exactly what to do but does not do it. These are people who feel they do not need God. Type Number Two knows and loves the Lord. These are people who will acknowledge Him and thank Him. Type Number Three knows they are the perfect Christian and view themselves as being on the fast track to heaven. These are the people who Rep His Name, the Jesus freaks.

Allow me to introduce Lake. He would line up with person number three. He, as well as Paul, is what you would call a track and field Christian, and the finish line is heaven. Lake walked up as Kim and Paul continued their conversation. Noticing the tension, he wanted to break the silence.

"Wow," Lake said after looking at Kim, "how are you this fine morning?" Turning to Paul with no enthusiasm at all, Lake said, "Hey, Wassup, Paul?"

Laughing, Kim said, "I'm doing pretty good this morning, Lake. How about yourself?"

"Oh, I'm great, homeward bound, lady," Lake said.

Lake put his head down and moved between Paul and Kim. He sat his book bag down and pulled out his cell phone. He noticed Tonya at the end of the building and said, "Kim, ain't that your girl Tonya down there with the prison-bound students of the school?"

"Wow, that was wrong, Lake," Kim said while laughing hysterically.

"It's wrong, but you are cracking up about it," Paul said shaking his finger in Kim's face, as if to say shame on you. "Please do not say something crazy that would make Kim want to go down there, Lake. You know how you are. You always manage to say that one thing that makes one of us want to touch your neck."

"You know that was funny though, Paul," Lake said while laughing. "But I feel you, that was wrong and bad timing."

Paul replied in a stern voice, "Yes, you do try to be funny, and it wouldn't be good if it happened because jail is not the place where you go to just hang out, eat in the food court, check out a movie, and go home, Lake. If I didn't know you outside of your crazy moments, I would not like you. You can be kind of suspect sometimes. Let us pray."

Lake said, "Oh my goodness, Paul, it's not that deep. Now why shouldn't she go down there? That's her friend. You mean if you saw me doing something that was jacked up, you would not say anything?"

Paul looked at Lake as if he had said something very stupid and rolled his eyes. "No, I would not." He smirked. "Real talk ya'll. That's some crazy mess Tonya is doing, and Kim does not need to go down there and say anything to her right now, period. As far as you are concerned, I would say something to you. But you have to understand that you are in a different place than she is spiritually; she's a *new* Christian. You cannot approach everybody the same way," Paul said adamantly. "How would you like it if someone approached you before you were ready to listen?

You have to feel out the situation, the atmosphere, check your spirit, or ask someone else to check theirs, if you are incapable at the time. Timing is everything, and every single situation is different, even if we refuse to accept that."

Kim paced the sidewalk with her hands on her head, very frustrated and trying to figure out why Tonya is choosing to hang with people who were not good for her. She said, "I'm all right, but y'all are wearin' me out right now. Here I am concerned about *my friend*. You know what, never mind. I'm not going down there, Paul. Chill out!"

"Why worry when we serve a God who knows all things and see's all things? Are you really going to put limitations on God when you know firsthand what He iscapable of?" Lake asked Kim.

Lake is not the type of person to mince words. He is very direct and to the point in everything that he does. His delivery is never rough or misdirected. He took off his glasses, put them in his pocket, and said, "Whatever it is, Kim, you need to give it to Him and let it go. Oh, and don't get it twisted. I'm not talking about Tonya. I'm talking about you."

"You're right, Lake, but that doesn't change the fact that I do want to go down there and pull my friend out of harm's way. A part of me feels like she's setting herself up to fail, whether intentionally or not."

Lake said in all sincerity, "You may be absolutely right, and you could be most assuredly wrong. Nevertheless, your words have power."

"Yeah, I know," Kim said.

"Then you know you must be very careful what you say whether about yourself or someone else. It's understandable," Lake continued to say, "that we want to rescue our friends. But, Kim, you have to understand that it is okay to want to be or need to be rescued. You have to think about you, too. Yes, you can help someone when you're going through. But you have to know when to go and when to not go. Most of all, you have to have the wisdom to know the difference. You know, people ask themselves from time to time, 'Why do I keep doing stupid stuff?' We know we are in the act of committing stupidity, but yet we still do it and then call ourselves stupid later for doing it. That's some crazy mess right there. But it is our mess, and we run to God to get us out of it later. Funny, isn't it?"

"Sometimes I have absolutely no idea what you are talking about, Lake. But as crazy as that was, I understood it. That was deep, man," Paul said with a smirk on his face.

"It's real talk though. Trust me. She knows there are things about those two that ain't right. As bumpy as the road will be, she will have to realize on her own that it's not for her to experience, consume, or endure. They don't need her help to be jacked up. She will find that out, hopefully, before something bad happens. They are going to see firsthand what you experience, consume, or endure by being connected to her," Paul said with much frustration in his voice.

Kim interrupted, "I hear you, though, Paul. All the same, I am going down there. I will be careful to make sure I don't put her on blast in front of them. But I need to know what is going on with her. I have to show her that I care and let her know she's not out here alone. I promise you, guys, I think something is going on with her. I can't put my finger on it, but it doesn't feel right to me.

There is more to this picture, and I want to go down there so I can find out what it is. Guys, really, she seemed broken, like she's got issues," Kim yelled. "You know the devil, one sign of weakness, and he's all over you. I will not allow my friend to experience that type of pain, not if I can help it."

Paul was curious as to how Tonya was acting at church the night before. He was sure that she was opening the shell and allowing God to break it layer by layer. Everything does not break off right away.

Paul turned and asked, "Lake, did you notice anything last night, at church? Lake! What are you doing? You can't just stand there like that and—"

"Let's get this right, 'kay, pumpkin. I could care less if they see me looking at them. They need to know, maybe then they will stop," Lake said. "Anyway, she was at church last night?" He put his head down for a moment to think. "Nah, not really." His head shook back and forth. "I was trying to get mine, so I don't know what anyone else was doing or not doing," Lake said, trying to be humorous.

"Help me, Lord!" Paul said clutching his chest.

"What's wrong with you?" Kim asked.

"I feel the spirit of slap coming over me in about three, two."

"Shut up, Paul, quit playing." Lake said pushing him so hard he fell on the ground.

"You two are crazy! Y'all argue like brothers. I'm gonna pray for both of you."

"All playing aside," Lake said, "I have been thinking about Tonya lately. I'm feeling like something is going on. I'm really hoping that I am wrong, but from the looks of it, I may not be. You don't want to push too hard though, Kim. If she is still as fragile as you say, you want to make sure you don't come off too strong. Talking to us and talking to her is totally different. Now, I'm not saying sugar coat the word, I'm just saying you don't want to say something that will push her over the edge or maybe even turn her onto them two."

Paul responds, "I'm sorry. Keep it real, Lake, which is something we all need to be doing right about now. What that girl needs, is a good old-fashioned whoopin'. Standing here talking about it, wishing, and hoping is not helping her. We know it's her down there. We know she's already turned on to them two, and we know she needs her butt whooped.

Someone really needs to lock her in a room somewhere. She knows what she needs to do and how she needs to act. It's not about comin' at her with scriptures. She needs that raw, in your face, or it's your life, love. And timing is everything."

Sarcastically Lake said, "Anyway, can I finish what I have to say, Paul? She has to make the choice of whose team she wants to be on, and it has to be on her own. Not just because you're her friend, Kim. Paul, don't you say one word," he turned and pointed. "Keep it to yourself."

Paul stood with his mouth open completely baffled. "That's all you had to say. You made it seem like you had so much more."

"Shut up, Paul," Lake said. "Would it just kill you to keep a smart comment to yourself? I'm just wondering. Hey, they're walking to the side of the building. You know people up to no good go on that side of the building. You should go be nosy, Kim."

"Lake, if you don't quit, I'm gonna feel more than a *spirit* of slap on me," Kim said.

"More like the spirit of homicide," Paul said.

"You feel me?" Kim said signifying.

"Kim, what you got goin' on later?" Paul asked.

Kim responded, "I don't have anything to do, so far. Why, Wassup?"

"I have to speak at this youth thing later. You should come hang out with me. What do you say?" Paul said persistently.

"Sure, I'll go with you. It will get me out of the house for a minute. Chloe drives me nuts sometimes. Do you want me to meet you there or what?" Kim questioned.

"Um, I can come get you. I'll be there around six. Cool?"

"Sure, I'll be ready. You just make sure you're not late. You know how you are." Kim said as she smacked Paul at the back of his neck.

"I'll be there on time. Be ready. I may stop and grab a bite. You good with that?" Paul added.

"Sure, Paul. Whatever you want to do," Kim said sarcastically.

Lake interjected, "I wanna go! No one asked if I wanted to go."

"You're right," Paul said.

"I'll see you guys at lunch," Kim said as she walked away. "I'm just going to go down there and say hello," she said softly.

Trying to get something started between Lake and Kim, Paul said, "Lake, you know, I think you let Kim off way too easy. You never asked what the problem was, what's going on, do you wanna talk—none of that. Why is that?"

Lake replies, "I didn't have to, Paul. If you want to know, then why don't you ask her? Or is it that you have, and she's not telling you anything? That was a rhetorical question. You don't have to know everything, Paul. I know you tell yourself that you do, however, I beg to differ. You do not."

Paul said a silent prayer as he watched Kim walk away. "Father God, I thank You for what You have given us and the flame that You have placed inside of us. I thank You for what You are about to do for Tonya and through Kim. I pray that Kim will be silent and that only You would speak. I call it done in Christ Jesus's name. Amen."

"Hey, see you later, shorty." Paul looked at Kim, and to make sure she stayed focused, he pointed with his finger to his head and his ear. He knew that this was a crucial moment of her and Tonya's friendship and hoped that Kim would choose the right thing to do.

"Paul, what are you about to do?" Lake asked.

"I'm going down here to talk to my new First Lady," Paul said as he laughed. "I don't know. She might not be ready for a preacher man like me. I'm the real deal. Then again, why would she pass up all this loveliness?"

"Wow, and you said that out loud."Lake stood there completely shocked. "What's really crazy is that you really believe it," Lake said in amazement. "I will continue to pray for you, Paul. Let me ask you something real quick."

"Hurry up, man, before my first lady leaves," Paul yelled.

"Why is it so hard for Kim to do what's right, and let this thing go with Tonya? She will be fighting a battle that she can't win on her own," Lake said.

Paul took a deep breath to really think about how to respond to the question. "I don't really know, man. She knows she's not in the position emotionally to walk up on Tonya, but she will anyway. As a Christian, as a woman, as a friend, she has to know what the right thing to do is and choose to do it.

You have to have a certain type of personality to hang with those two," Paul said as he pointed down to Leah and Tim. "So, I know Tonya may not be receptive to being walked up on, let alone to being questioned. Kim is a strong young lady who cares for all her friends. That's why she's a friend of mine."

Paul's mind drifted in another direction as his eyes followed Kim, walking toward Tonya.

"Where did you go, man? I know you have feelings for Kim. Does she know?" Lake asked Paul.

"No, she does not, and you better not say one word to her. And I mean it. We are friends, and that's it. Kim is not ready for someone like me," Paul said arrogantly.

"Are *you* ready for someone like Kim, is the question." Lake said. "I think not, 'cause Kim ain't no joke, man. I don't know what you're talkin' about. Kim's got mind, body, soul, meaning she is bad. You better quit playin'. You can walk around here like it's her that ain't ready. Nah, man, it's you. She may be going through something right now, but don't get it twisted. That's a strong young lady."

Lake bent down to pick up his book bag to go inside the school. "I'll get at you later. Go catch up with your 'new first lady,' 'cause that down there is a preacher, and she's not easily influenced or swayed," he said as he laughed, shook his head, and walked away.

CHAPTER SUMMARY

At what cost? At what cost do we continue to take matters into our own hands, when we know there is someone who can handle any situation. That is the question to be asked. At some point we all must learn for ourselves what is right and what is wrong. It is one thing to not want to leave your loved one out in the cold to fend for their self but is another thing to push them to the point of no return because you do not want to wait on God. At whose expense does a concerned friend continue to try and dictate the path of another? When will we turn it over to God and let Him lead the way?

Kim had made up in her mind that she was going to confront Tonya. A lot of times, we forget that we have no control over our friends' issues, what they say or do. In our role as a friend, we tend to do things that could make our relationships unpleasant. The only thing we can do is give them to God and let Him repair what is broken.

More often than not, our bad habits do not come off right away. Nothing changes until we allow the Word to come in to renew and restore; then and only then, will the walls begin to come down. We must always remember that change does not happen right away. It is easy to react out of anger or fear. It is not as easy for a person to wait and hear from God before choosing to react. When will we say enough is enough of choosing the wrong thing? When do we begin to allow God to take the wheel? Do we continue to choose to operate on our own, making choices outside the plan of God is not possible in the life of a Christian? The way Kim handles this situation would make all the difference in the world concerning Tonya. The love of a friend is special, and to have a friend that will go to war for you is an awesome thing. But when does it click that only God can change certain aspects of a situation, fix, or deliver? It was especially important that Kim listen clearly to God in order to make the right choices. But what is the right choice?

Is it to walk away and let God handle it? Is it to confront him or her? We as friends can have the best intentions. Nevertheless, ifwe approach the situation with a foul attitude, not waiting until after we calm down, not allowing God to tell us what to do and say, the wanting to help turns into a full-blown firestorm. Consider this scripture:

"So if you know of an opportunity to do the right thing today, yet you refrain from doing it, you're guilty of sin."

James (Jacob) 4:17 TPT

Some may say, "I'm not saved, I don't know God. Simply put, I do not go to church. I don't know what sin is and what it is not." But what about when you get that funny feeling in the pit of your stomach, and something does not feel right deep down inside? That means at that very moment it is not the right thing to do. We generally know the difference between nervous knots and the *this is not right feeling*. We must at least try to distinguish the difference and do the right thing. We cannot allow our loneliness, our need to be liked or appreciated, and/or our desire to seek the approval of another to continue to influence us to make bad choices.

In everything that we do, we must always be an influence and not be easily influenced by the things of this world.

"But the fruit produced by the Holy Spirit within you is divine love in all its varied expressions: joy that overflows, peace that subdues, patience that endures, kindness in action, a life full of virtue, faith that prevails, gentleness of heart, and strength of spirit. Never set the law above these qualities, for they are meant to be limitless. As youyield freely and fully to the dynamic life and powerof the Holy Spirit, you will abandon the cravingsof your self-life. For your self-life craves the thingsthat offend the Holy Spirit and hinder him from living free within you! And the Holy Spirit's intense cravings hinder your old self-life from dominating you! So then, the two incompatible and conflicting forces within you are your self-life of the flesh and the new creation life of the Spirit. But when you are brought into the full freedom ofthe Spirit of grace, you will no longer be living under the domination of the law, but soaring above it!

The cravings of the self-life are obvious: Sexual immorality, lustful thoughts, pornography, chasing after things instead of God, manipulating others, hatred of those who get in your way, senseless arguments, resentment when others are favored, temper tantrums, angry quarrels, only thinking of yourself, being in love with your own opinions, being envious of the blessings of others, murder, uncontrolled addictions, wild parties, and all other similar behavior. Haven't I already warned youthat those who use their "freedom" for these things will not inherit the kingdom realm of God!"

Galatians 5:16-23 TPT

CHAPTER THREE

Now we see Jeff, a PK—*preacher's kid*. He is Type Number Two, type of Christian and he is on the verge of losing his way. He knows what is expected of him, yet he chooses his own way. His father is the pastor of a major church in the city. His main concern is being the popular kid in school and in his place of worship. He is convinced that he is able to maintain his Christianity no matter what he does, and he runs with the wrong group of people.

None of his friends are in church. Jeff is not willing to stay focused and balanced, and he does not care. As long as he plays the drums, helps his father from time to time, and runs the streets just the way he likes, he's cool. He refuses to further his knowledge, and subsequently, he is in danger of losing his soul. The thought of this will never enter his mind because he does not care. No matter what the age, there are individuals whose thoughts are not on God. If you identify with him, I pray that by the end of this book, you choose another way.

Jeff was excited to see Kim, to the point where he could not contain himself. He ran up behind her, threw his arms around her, and yelled, "What's up, girl? What you doing? Where are you going, Kim?"

"Dag-on it, Jeff, you scared me!" Kim screamed pushing him away from her. "What do you want for crying out loud?" With a death grip, she clutched her bag, glared at him, and said, "Shouldn't you beon your way to class to get on your teacher's nerves and not mine?"

"Why are you walking this way?" Jeff yelled. "Your class is on the other side of the building."

As you can see, Jeff is very persistent. He does not like rejection, and he is not very comfortable with being ignored. It makes you wonder if there is some underlying issue with Jeff. Think about it. His father being who he is, he spends most of his time in church, majority of the time unwillingly or in the streets. It could be that Jeff's father is not able to spend time with him alone, but he does not complain because that is the perfect time to run the streets, when his father is occupied with the church. The reason Jeff does not want to change his lifestyle lies within him.

Kim rolled her eyes and began walking faster, hoping he would get the point or just walk away. "I'm trying to catch up with my friend, and you always seem to pick the worst times to say hello. In your own special way, I might add."

"Okay, I'll give you that," Jeff said."Who are you talking about, Tonya?"

"Yes, I'm talking about Tonya. What can I help you with Jeff?" Kim said as she pictured herself hitting Jeff over the head with her bag.

Jeff had this knack of getting under Kim's skin. He jumped in front of her to slow her down. "You know I don't like her at all."

"That's funny because I don't recall asking you if you did or even caring for that matter," Kim said.

"Well, that wasn't very nice, Kim," Jeff replied. "You are always so nasty to me. I think we should talk about that, don't you?"

"Um, what I think we should talk about is how painful it would be if I hit you with my bag. I don't have time for this right now, Jeff. I'll talk to you later," Kim said as she laughed and walked away.

Jeff jumped in front of Kim once more and shouted, "Oh, really, Kim?"

Kim stopped, threw her hands up in frustration, and a thought of laying hands on him really hard came to mind. Kim thought to herself, *this is not happening to me*. "Jeff, you can't be serious. Really, what—what in the world could you possibly want?"

With piercing eyes, the quiver on the left side of her lip, and beads of sweat on her forehead from anger, Kim gave Jeff a look that even scared him. He backed up because he knew he had pushed Kim to her limit.

Afraid to answer the question, Jeff replied hesitantly, "You'll talk to me later?"

"Yes, Jeff!" Kim yelled. "Please! I don't have time for this. I have to catch up with Tonya! You better hope and pray I did not miss her."

"Fine then, Kim, keep walking. I don't know why I even try, and you wonder why I . . . whatever," Jeff said as he walked away.

Kim was annoyed beyond belief by Jeff and his willingness to be completely vexing. Jeff had tried from time to time to get Kim's attention, not caring that he was rubbing her the wrong way. He has wanted to hang out with her for a very long time. However, Kim would never give him the time of day.

Aware of the type of people Jeff ran with and not understanding why, Kim kept her distance. Kim did not want to be associated with that type of person and drama. Kim was completely pissed off at Jeff to the point where she would have run him over with her car if she could. She stomped down the sidewalk toward Tonya trying her best to calm down before she got there. Knowing that as irritated as she was, if someone said something crazy to her, she would lose her mind. Hoping Jeff had not caused her to miss Tonya, Kim walked a little faster.

Kim thought to herself, *this is for crap! Why is she doing this to herself? Where are her parents? This is their job! I have my own issues to deal with. Why do I feel so responsible for her? I didn't tell her to smoke and hang out with horrible people. But if I ignore it and don't say anything and something happens to her, I would never forgive myself. Okay, I had to vent for a minute.* Breathing in and out, *woos a, woos a,* she said. *Now that I got that out, I can do this and like it. Oh, Lord, this doesn't look good at all. Please give me the words to say. Help me to get out of my own way so that You can have the final say. What is she doing with them, Lord?*

I know I don't need to understand. You do and that is all that matters because You are in control not me. This is all about You Father.

After what felt like the longest walk ever, Kim caught up with Tonya and her new friends Tim and Leah. Kim glanced in Tonya's direction, well aware that Tonya could see her standing there. Kim noticed the look of shame on Tonya's face as she held her head down.

Just a thought, if you feel ashamed about what you are doing, it is an indication you should not be doing it. Both Tim and Leah have very bad reputations around town, and everyone in school knew that to be true. How Kim handles this situation remains to be seen. Tim is a runner for the biggest drug dealer in the city, and Leah has the disposition of a follower and frequently makes runs with Tim. Not only does Kim have to be an influence on Tonya, but she must be to Tim and Leah as well. She cannot allow her feelings and judgment of Tim and Leah to get in the way of what she is called to do, and that is to be a positive influence.

Tonya never acknowledged Kim, and that began to upset her even more. "What's up? Why y'all over here?" Kim asked as she watched Tim and Leah pass a joint.

"We're trying not to be seen, what you think we're doing?" Leah said in a nasty tone.

She'd better be glad I'm saved, Kim said to herself. *Tonya, you can't speak, devil got your tongue?"*

"Oh, hi Kim. I'm sorry I didn't see you standing there. How are you doing?" Not able to think of another lie, Tonya turned her head to look at Tim. The last thing she needed was him trying to pass it to her, in front of Kim.

Kim knew the answer to the question she was about to ask, but she decided to ask anyway. "Hmm, okay. Did you get your paper done for English class last night, Tonya?"

"Well, I . . . Tonya said.

While laughing and choking on smoke, Tim interrupted Tonya by trying to insinuate she was doing something else. "I know what she was doing last night, and it wasn't an English paper."

"Better yet *who* she was doing," Leah interjected.

Tonya responded, "Whatever, what I do in my private time is my business, not the two of yours. Besides neither one of you can talk or put anyone on blast out here."

"Don't put it out there if you don't want people to know," Tim said.

"Shut up Tim. I don't think I was talking to you." Putting one finger to her mouth to think about it, she stopped, pointed at him and said. "Hmm, no. I'm sure I wasn't."

"Why should he shut up Tonya? If it's such a big secret, keep it to yourself," Leah said.

Feeling very convicted and ashamed at that moment, Tonya stood quietly, looking down at the ground and showing no emotion.

"I know a lot of your secrets, Leah, so don't start. You absolutely don't want none." Tonya said.

"I thought you guys were friends. Dang, y'all talk to each other like you can't stand one another," Kim said.

"Anyway, you are the only one pretending to be something you're not, Tonya," Tim said. "Or is it that you just don't want your church friend to know?" Tim looked at Tonya, knowing he had something to hide and had no right to talk about her the way he did.

"Whatever leave me alone," Tonya said as she pushed Tim and nearly knocked him off his feet. "Like I said, neither one of you can talk, especially you, Tim. *And*, Leah, you know I know all your secrets. Back off!" Tonya yelled at the top of her lungs.

Jeff found it very amusing to sneak up behind Kim and bump into her as he and his friends walked by.

Kim turned to look at him and said, "Excuse me would work, Jeff. Oh God, he touched me!" Kim said as she wiped off her arm. "Tonya!" Kim yelled. Before she knew it, Tonya was gone. "Where did she go that quickly? Thanks a *lot*, Jeff," she said. *Lord, I know that we should love everybody, but did You really mean Jeff too?"* The thought immediately popped into her mind.

"What's crackin', church girl?" Leah asked as she tapped Kim on the shoulder. "You wanna hit?"

Kim paused for a moment and tried to figure out why Leah would ask her that question and responded, "Now, tell me how church girl and weed have anything in common, Leah?" Kim shook her head and rolled her eyes at Leah. "Do you guys know where Tonya went?"

"She said she was going to the bathroom, but if you ask me, she probably headed for the cafeteria to get something to eat on," Tim said in a sarcastic manner.

"Kim, you sure you don't wanna hit this? Come on, you don't know what you're missing. It's some good stuff," Leah said.

"What did you not understand? Think about that question, Leah, and then think about asking me again," Kim said. "This makes absolutely no sense to me." Shaking her head, Kim thought to herself, *she doesn't need any more weed. It's making her dumber by the minute. Lord, can we add Leah and Tim to that list with Jeff, too? Sike, I'm just playin'.*

"Hey, Kim, when you see Tonya, tell her to come here for a minute. That would be most helpful to me, please and thank you," Tim said.

Kim hesitated for a second and said, "Yeah, sure."

When you least expect it, you will come in contact with someone that does know the Lord, does have, or had a relationship with Him. Everything that Kim stands for, Paul reps, and Lake strives to be, Tim has already done and more. Tim was once able to see things in the spirit that not many people he once called friend, were able to. Tim was a Christian rapper who found himself in a situation that led him to a world he's not equipped to live in. He was easily influenced by someone who took advantage of him. It should make you think about your own life. This particular story may not apply to you.

Nevertheless, there may be that one thing that makes you hurt all over. It throws off your judgment, and you become vulnerable. In turn, you begin to act outside of yourself. This is where a strong relationship with The Lord comes to play.

Just take a moment to think about your life. Know it is always good to make the best positive choice, but there may have been a time when you didn't or couldn't. God's grace is greater, and He gave you a gift of forgiveness through Jesus Christ. Oftentimes, forgiveness is not about forgiving others, it is forgiving yourself, as well.

CHAPTER SUMMARY

It is hard to release your grip of control, trust me, I know. No matter what lies we hear, whether from ourselves or someone else, we must not be easily swayed. Let God's love change you from the inside out. You never want to climb a mountain alone, nor do you want to experience uncharted territory, alone. Think about it; without a covering, you are walking alone. Whether the covering be a Spiritual Mother, Father, or church home, everyone needs that. Listen, we all need someone to call for prayer or spiritual wisdom and guidance.

We can never forget that our friends cannot get the message needed if we are spiritually weak. Healing needs to take place from within. How can you be used by God, minister, or evangelize if you are spiritually weak? Not gonna happen, not if you want it to be affective. People we encounter, are blessed in our overflow. Know that we are not in the position, mentally, to confront or be a comfort to anyone.

Why do we continue to fight battles we cannot win on our own? We set ourselves up to fail when we do anything unprotected. Never be easily influenced or react out of your pain, hurt and confusion.

Disregarding what she needed to do for herself, Kim made a beeline in Tonya's direction. Being the hardcore Christian that Kim is, her mission is to serve the Lord with all her heart and to live her life for Him, no matter what the cost. Straddling the fence was no longer an option for Kim. We must touch God and all that He is for ourselves and not because of someone else. Let me share something else with you. There are those who live and talk to God because of who they know and not because of their love for Him. Attending worship services becomes more of a habit or routine. You must understand, truly knowing The Lord is not just about going through the motions. I say that because, as a true Believer, you must have your own personal relationship with The Lord. The type of relationship where you seek Him out before doing anything. Before making a move, you check with Him first.

When something exciting happens in your life, you tell Him first. This may sound extreme, but trust me when I tell you, sometimes extreme is what is needed. When your fleshly desire tries to creep in, you pause and think first, it will help you to not sin. There is conviction. Why, because you have a yearning to always want to be in His Will. Why, because of your love for Him. That love helps you not to sin.

Check it, I tell my mommy everything. Good or bad, like clockwork. I try by best not to disappoint my parents and represent them well. Why, because they are my parents and that is what daughters should do. The relationships that you have today are with people you talk to often and spend time with. Your relationship with God should be ten times stronger than that of a mother and a father. It is a vital part of your life as a Christian. Here is a scripture to consider:

"So let it be the same way with you! Since you are now joined with him, you must continually view yourselves as dead and unresponsive to sin's appeal while living daily for God's pleasure in union with Jesus, the Anointed One. Sin is a dethroned monarch; so you must no longer give it an opportunity to rule over your life, controlling how you live and compelling you to obey its desires and cravings. So then, refuse to answer its call to surrender your body as a tool for wickedness. Instead, passionately answer God's call to keep yielding your body to him as one who has now experienced resurrection life! You livenow for his pleasure, ready to be used for hisnoble purpose. Remember this: sin will not conquer you, for God already has! You are not governed by law but governed by the reign of the grace of God."

Romans 6:11-14 TPT

It is catastrophic to our relationship with God when we give in to sin and not obey Him. You must at all times try to not sin. Trust and believe, the devil will try to trip you up. The stronger the relationship, the easier it gets. At some point in our lives,whether a Christian or not, we must stop and think, are our actions a good or bad influence on someone else. Hopefully, that concerns you. Believe it or not, the way you respond to things, the people around you, overlooking the precious moments that God wants to show you, will keep you from the blessings that are meant for you and put you in harm's way. Do not miss out on those things because you react first.

Tonya was torn between two different lifestyles because of her desire to be liked by Tim and his friends, which meant Leah. She was willing to put the need to satisfy her flesh before her relationship with God. Tonya wanted nothing more than to stifle whatever Tim and Leah could possibly say in front of other people.

Let me add, if you are ashamed to let people know, then you ought not do it. Kim had no idea where Tonya's friendship with Tim and Leah stood. All Kim really had to go by was her perception of Tim and Leah. Let me also add, it is not cool to judge people. Tonya feels that what she does with her time is her business, which is a true belief. Tonya had the constant reminder that Kim introduced her to the Lord. Any decision that you make after accepting Jesus into your heart is between you and Him. Not you, Him, and everyone else. Hence, *your* relationship and walk with The Lord.

All too often, we are more concerned with ducking, dodging, and hiding, not realizing someone is watching and observing when we do wrong. Our obligation, our loyalty, and our concern should be to the One who gave us life.

Some may not care. They may not be concerned because they feel it is not necessary to know the Lord. Again, I pray that by the end of this book, their minds have changed.

When you think about life, what do you think about? How do you view your life? Ask yourself these questions, and when doing so, remember it is vital to your life naturally and spiritually. That was just a little side note for you.

Isn't it funny how we never want to admit our guilt when we are caught with our hand in the cookie jar, so to speak? What do we do? We stand there perfectly still and catch the "it wasn't me syndrome," while thinking of something to say. Could our eyes get any bigger? Take a moment and think about certain aspects of your life and the choices that you have made. We have allowed ourselves to be influenced by our friends. We do things we would not normally do on our own, at the same time wishing, things were done differently. Not recognizing, at the time, that our choices can affect the rest of our lives.

Keep in mind, our words have power. The way we speak can change the heart and mind of an individual. It is extremely important that we are not influenced by negative surroundings, or people—namely friends and their lifestyles. These things can easily influence how we think, what we say, and what we do. Are you strong enough to not permit those things to influence you? Take this seriously. Your life has purpose, it has meaning.

We cannot afford to give in to things that may take our eyes off God. Once we accept Him into our lives, we can be changed into the man or woman He has called us to be, but we have to allow Him to. God can change the way we think, the way we live, and the way we carry ourselves. There are so many things calling for our attention and trying to take our focus off the right things. If we are not careful and strong enough, we will be influenced by things that are not of God. We must choose to be an influence and not be influenced. Countless Christians have lost their way, and, at the same time, countless unsaved individuals are trying to find their way. In both instances it can get difficult to fight. Things get in the way, whether they be issues, friends, family, or other elements of life.

These things keep us from choosing a straight path. Nine times out of ten, it is not that we do not want to give everything over to God, but it may be hard for us to do so, and God knows that. That is why He has put things in place to keep us on track. One of those things is the Word of God.

In *1 Corinthians 10:13, He tells you that no matter what, you can endure.* You may be fighting unforgiveness or not being able to release certain things or people. In the prison of our minds reside whatever it is that is keeping us from truly being free. What is the reason you have not chosen? Don't you think it is time? Tonya has chosen another way, and Kim will stand in the gap for her. While those are standing in the gap for someone in need, we must remind ourselves not to judge and accuse.

Always understand, the same measure you use will be measured to you by God. Believer or non-believer, it is not cool to judge anyone, whether they are a believer or a non-believer. Leave that to the One who knows all and sees all. Trust me, He has all the answers.

CHAPTER FOUR

Shortly after she entered the school building, Kim noticed Tonya sitting in the hallway on the floor. Tonya knew she would be looking for her eventually, so there was no point in hiding. Looking through her book bag, Tonya kept her head down, just in case Kim walked down the hall. At the other end of the hallway, Kim stood trying to figure out whether she wanted to speak to Tonya. A couple of minutes went by, and Kim decided to say hello.

Kim said to herself, *now, this right here is out of my control. And I'm not sure what to do. I know me. She's gonna push me, and it won't be pretty. She knows You Lord.* Kim closed her eyes and calmed her breathing before she started down the hallway. She approached Tonya and waited to speak. With a soft yet serious tone, Kim asked, "What's up Tonya?"

Without looking up, not wanting to give a vocal response, Tonya shook her head.

Tonya decided to ask Kim a question she wasn't expecting. "Before you even get it in on me, let me ask you. Did you forget that I know you, too?"

Kim stood with a very surprised look on her face, not responding right away.

"Don't walk up on me and think you're gonna come at me crazy. I'm really good with you right now, to tell you the truth," Tonya stressed to Kim.

Kim did not expect Tonya to come at her the way she was, and right out the gate. Trying not to get upset, Kim said, "Is that right?"

"Yeah that's right, Kim. I'm tired, and I don't want to deal with your judgment today," Tonya said. "Didn't expect me to come at you, did you? I am not going to let you talk to me crazy, so . . ."

"So, what Tonya?" Kim asked.

Tonya said, "Let this go and leave me alone."

"Judgment? What are you talking about? I never judged you! Oh, okay, my being concerned about you, that's what you consider judging?" Kim replied without hiding her annoyance.

"I think you're more concerned because you like being in somebody else's business. You just can't leave well enough alone. That's too much like right. Take care of your own issues," Tonya said.

"You have been smoking, haven't you? Do you think you're old enough to handle the psychological aspect that comes along with smoking? Evidently not because you're doing it at school. Don't you know that your body is the temple of the Holy Spirit, who lives in you and was given to you by God? I can just imagine what else you are doing. You don't belong to yourself, for God bought you with a price. So, you must honor God with your body," Kim said.

"What are you talking about, Kim? I thought you were walking away. No—ya know what, I don't want to know." Tonya picked up her comb and brush, put them back in her bag and began to get up to walk away from Kim.

The more Tonya made excuses; the more annoyed Kim became. In frustration, Kim said to Tonya, "I'm talking about you and this mess you're connected to."

Tonya dropped her head, followed by a deep sigh. "Yeah, if I didn't know it before, I know it now. You don't know me at all. Why do you care about who I spend my time with and what I do when I'm with them? Christians kill me looking down on people as if they didn't come out the womb a sinner."

"Obviously, I don't know you," Kim said looking Tonya up and down. "I'm talking about what you are doing to yourself. What I'm talking about Tonya is you hanging out with two of the most..." Giving up on trying to find diplomatic words, Kim threw up her hands and said, "Look, why are you friends with them?"

"That's none of your business," Tonya said.

"It's clear they do not respect you Tonya. Look at how they were talking to you outside. I'm telling you, something is not right here, and for some reason, you refuse to see it. Maybe it's because you don't want to. Maybe there is a deeper reason, and we will know it very soon."

Tonya put her things down and got real up close and personal with Kim. The look on her face did not seem like the Tonya Kim was used to. "You need to back up off me. So what? I didn't stay to talk to you. Dang, I had to come inside to do something, and I didn't want to be late for class. You're really starting to tick me off." Tonya wanted nothing more than to shut Kim down, and it took everything in her to not punch her in her mouth.

Kim backed up and shook her head in amazement. A very confused Kim said, "There is still another fifteen minutes 'til class starts, Tonya." She leaned back on the locker, silently braced herself, and waited for Tonya's next response. Atthis point, Kim knew this conversation was not going to go as planned.

"Whatever. Secondly, I'm not doing anything to myself that I don't want to happen. What makes you think everything you do is the right thing? So, you decided to judge what I do as bad and what you do as the right thing?"

"I beg to differ on that, Tonya. I'm not doing what you think I'm doing. But me standing here telling you that is not good enough. You're just straight defensive, and I'm supposed to take it because it's you. I don't think so. Two point two seconds, and this could be all bad. I'm choosing to back up," Kim said. "Don't get it twisted."

"Thirdly, I can smoke whatever I want, when I want, and hang out with whoever I want. You do not own me, and I'm starting to rethink my friendship with you! Keep backing up on that," Tonya said.

It's been a long time since Kim had to lay into someone, and she thought this might quickly happen. Kim could feel her neck getting hot, and her heartbeat was extremely fast. She waited and took a deep breath. "Jesus," she said softly. Clutching the strap on her bag, she took one step toward Tonya and said in a soft tone, "Clearly, and you do that very well. Why can't you see that this type of lifestyle is not good for you? If they want to ruin their lives, let them. Tonya, this road you are taking is crooked and is not for you. What's up with you?"

"What do you mean? I'm good. Why are you so worried about what's going on with me? You need to worry about yourself. I don't need your help, Kim."

Tonya is clearly trying to push Kim's buttons, and it is possible that Kim will respond in a way that Tonya never expects as well.

"I said I'm fine, Kim, get up off me. I always bounce back." Tonya said and tried to walk away.

"That's just it, Tonya. God doesn't want you to just bounce back. He wants you to be able to stand. Yes, we may fall every now and then. He knows that. He's all knowing. But you have to know that He is here for you. So, you don't have to go through whatever you're going through alone. I'm sorry. I'm just concerned, that's all. God loves you, and He wants nothing but the best for you. I know you know that."

With great emotion Tonya said, "I know this is hard for you to grasp, Kim, but it's not that simple! My life is not centered around you. I got some grown-up issues going on right now. I just need time. I'm not ready yet, and I don't want to deal with you, too! But you refuse to see that or accept it."

"Not ready? Not ready for what, Tonya? What are you waiting on, something drastic to happen? What are you going through? Not ready! What is there to think about? God didn't second-guess giving you life. Do we need to watch *The Passion* again, girl? Do you need to be reminded of the fact that Jesus loves you and how much He went through because of that love? You were ready last week, what makes you not ready this week? Aren't you glad I'm not God?"

"I said I'm not ready, Kim. Now, for the last time, back the heck up." Tonya said and pointed her finger toward Kim's face.

Kim took another deep breath and smacked Tonya's hand out of her face. "You don't want none of this! Two point two seconds and things could potentially be all bad for you," Kim said. "Keep your hand out of my face. You know what? It would give me much pleasure to throw your little butt up and down this hall, however, I'm not gonna do that. Let me say this to you and then I'm going to walk away before I do something that will completely rip our friendship apart."

"If not already," Tonya said.

"Yeah, whatever then," Kim yelled. "One of the awesome things about God is that He allows you to choose whether you want to give your life completely to Him or not. When you are ready, He will be waiting for you, with open arms. You know what else is amazing? He's still right behind you and on each side of you while you're in your 'not readiness,' and He won't hold it against you."

"You just don't get it, Kim! Leave me alone," Tonya screamed. "Better yet, when I walk away from you, don't ever talk to me. I got a lot going on, and trust me, you are not helping. You're too busy scolding me, instead of asking me what the issue is."

"Don't get it twisted, Tonya. I do get it. That's what you don't understand. I was where you are right now. Not ready to be completely sold out for God, not willing to give up myself, my will. I get it."

"You know, Kim, if you did get it, you would back the heck off! You suck at being a friend. Part of being a friend is to know when to do just that. I'm real close to treating you like an enemy."

Tonya walked away from Kim and went back outside with Leah and Tim.

"Okay, that went well," Kim said sarcastically. "I know she hates me now, for sure. It wasn't supposed to go that way. Lord, please help Tonya. Better luck next time. If I get a next time." she said.

Kim may have lost whatever opportunity she had to speak in Tonya's life. Things of this nature happen all the time. You have an argument with someone, and it completely tears your friendship apart. Why? After looking back at the situation, was it worth it? Be the one to get up and walk away if the other person does not.

When you are upset, things can be said that you cannot take back. Remember your words have power. Please be conscious of the words that you say and the way you say them.

CHAPTER SUMMARY

Being left in the hallway by herself after that explosive encounter, was devastating to Kim, and that was not supposed to happen. Certain that Tonya would never talk to her again, Kim would never get another moment to really do what needed to be done. After it was all said and done, Kim still did not realize, her timing was jacked up. Sometimes we need to just stop, pray, and listen before reacting. Things would have gone a lot smoother if Kim had waited on God. Not to mention, Tonya made it very clear that she did not want to deal with Kim at that moment, but Kim decided to continue the conversation. Yes, it was one that needed to be had, however that was not the time or place. We, as people, must know when to leave well enough alone. We have to know when to walk away. When to stop and when to go, safely and freely. We must have better judgment, in each and every situation. There is something to say for the wisdom Kim had received from Paul and Lake just twenty minutes beforehand.

Once she saw Tonya was not in the mood for a conversation of that magnitude, Kim should have stopped. In all honesty, if you must take a deep breath because of your frustration, why even begin. Due to poor judgment on Kim's part, the conversation took a wrong turn. Kim had about enough of the way Tonya was acting. Kim felt as though she had all the right intentions when she approached Tonya. This is an example of why you should not act alone. Tonya was in defense mode well before Kim walked down the hall. Because of that, Tonya would take offense to anything Kim said. Your frustration about another issue in your life can cause you to lash out at someone else.

There had never been a time when Kim was not able to have a conversation with Tonya. Tonya is well aware that the life she is living is not what God had in mind. Never forget that the power of the flesh is strong, and if you do not have divine help, it will be tough. Tough to resist him or her, tough to resist that drink or another hit. We need to get out of the world's rotation and get realigned with the Lord.

It is easy to fall into that trap of authorizing the things of the world to become an idol, trust me I know, and that is Not okay with God. No matter the reason, we need to get it together.

Kim must remember that we are not fighting against flesh and blood, but against evil rulers and authorities of the unseen world, against mighty powers in this dark world, and against evil spirits in the heavenly places. We must also remember that the devil is fighting us and that we must always keep a watchful eye and our spirit strong.

Tonya walked away crying, angry, and confused. After that very intense, very emotional conversation, she was ready to throw her friendship with Kim away. She felt as though she was being judged and looked upon in a negative way. One of the things she admired about Kim was her compassion toward other people, but Tonya had not felt it that day. We are never to judge another individual, however, we all do, whether intentionally or not. There are some who make many judgments every day. A good scripture to consider:

"Refuse to be a critic full of bias toward others, and judgment will not be passed on you. For you'llbe judged by the same standard that you've used

to judge others. The measurement you use on them will be used on you."
Matthew 7:1-2 TPT

We as Christians do not realize our actions and our choice to correct, be it another Christian or non-Christian, can be portrayed as judgmental or condescending. Keeping in mind that whatever measure is used in judging others will be used to measure how we are judged. We must not react to a situation without seeking God and waiting for a release to speak or act.

How would you have handled this situation? How many times have you wished for a do-over? Having a true friendship with someone is a powerful element of life. We have the awesome opportunity to share, care, love, and to touch the lives of those we have friendships with. It is extremely important that we are incredibly careful with how and what we speak to or about another human being.

After the confrontation, Kim stood amazed but not in a good way. She had allowed her emotions to take over.

This is something that we are all guilty of, giving in to our flesh and emotions in a negative way; yelling, not listening to one another, and not being willing to compromise is a recipe for a bad relationship or friendship. Take your time and wait to confront the issue at hand.

Weighing heavy on her mind, Kim questioned her decision to talk to Tonya and if she handled it the right way. Everything that Paul told her hit her like an out-of-control freight train. No one is perfect, and no one will handle every situation perfectly. This is why it is important to seek God before reacting.

CHAPTER FIVE

It is the day after the most tragic, most catastrophic event in her life, or so Kim thought. Kim arrived at the school counselor's office, to complete her office hours. Filled with a gamut of emotions, she tried her best to no longer think about her conversation with Tonya. Mrs. Karns was exceptionally good at pulling things out of people without breaking a sweat. Mrs. Karns has gotten to know numerous students, along with their behavior, so Kim was sure she would figure something out. Kim collected her thoughts, knocked on the door, and patiently waited to be welcomed in.

"Good morning, Mrs. Karns. How are you today?" Kim said as she entered the room.

"Well hello there Kim. It's been a long morning already, and it just got started.How are you? What's been up with you? I haven't seen you in a while. You guys went out of town for your family reunion, right?" Mrs. Karns said.

"Yes, we went to South Carolina last week, but I was here yesterday, though. I should have just taken the day and stayed home, but I decided to come anyway. I don't know how mommy pulled that off with me and school. Lord knows I'm gonna have a lot of homework to do. On top of everything else I must worry about, now I have that. What to be concerned about first," Kim said in a serious tone. "Anyway, I'm good. Is there anything you need me to do? I can finish where I left off the time I was here if you would like."

Without looking up, she became the busy little bee and got to work. With hopes Mrs. Karns would not notice she was out of sorts, Kim stood with her back turned.

"It would be great if you could go through those files on the bookshelf. When you have completed what you're doing, look at those files there and make sure the dates match. The last four of the phone number need to match, and the last names need to match as well. Once you're done with that, you can put them in alphabetical order. I must get ready for the conferences tomorrow. Aren't you glad you're almost done with school?"

"Yes and no. I have so much to think about," Kim said.

"Yes, you do, and you will get it done. Everything you set out to do will be completed, and all your decisions will begood ones. You cannot continue to second-guess yourself. You'll be fine, Kim. Why don't you go to the school we recently talked about and keep it moving? Now, what else is bothering you?"

Mrs. Karns knew there was more to the equation, and Kim refused to say a word. Kim picked up the files and sat down by the window.

"I have some colleges in mind, but I haven't made my decision yet."

"You're getting down to the wire. You should have made that decision months ago. The reason you have not made a choice is because you're thinking about not attending college. Snap out of that, now." Mrs. Karns said.

"Yes, I need to make up my mind soon," Kim replied.

"Not soon, but now." Mrs. Karns added.

"I'm narrowing it down. I just don't want to leave my mom and Chloe. I know I shouldn't base my decision on that. It's just on my mind. If I stay close that's cool. If I go, that's cool, too," Kim said. "Would you like me to file them away, as well?" Kim asked and pointed at a stack of files.

"Yes, sort through them there. Put the yellow papers in these folders. Thank you. Well, what do you like most about those schools?"

"I love the campuses of all of them. The classes will be challenging but rewarding at the same time. I like that I have the option of studying abroad, but I don't know about those," she said as she pointed at each of them. "Of these two here, one is less expensive but they're both out of town," Kim said.

"I guess you've made your decision," Mrs. Karns said with a smile on her face.

"I guess I did. But I would have to move away, and I don't know how to feel about that. This one would be my first pick, but I still don't know what to do."

It was the first time Kim had really sat down to weigh her options on colleges. She realized she is more concerned about her mother and sister than herself.

"Kim, you know what I'm going to say. You cannot base your decision of colleges on family. Your mother is an awesome woman and mother. Trust that she knows what she is doing with Chloe. She did with you. You are a smart and beautiful young lady, inside and out. Your future is bright, and you have to believe that whatever choice you make will be a great one. Excuse me for a minute," Mrs. Karns said.

Mrs. Karns stepped out to meet with the principal. While she was gone, Kim was able to think more about her choice and what her mother would say. When Mrs. Karns returned, she noticed Kim staring at the wall with a blank look on her face and showing no emotion. She stood in the doorway for a few moments trying to figure out what was going through Kim's mind. Several seniors in the school have that same look and disposition this time of year. Their high school years are ending and turning the tassel marks the beginning of their adult college life. Some know their next step, and some do not. However, Mrs. Karns only knows part of Kim's dilemma. The pressures of being a senior and thinking about colleges and her family were not the only things on Kim's mind.

Kim quickly began working as Mrs. Karns stepped back into the office. Minutes went by and a roar of complete silence came over the room.

"Kim what is going on with you?" Mrs. Karns said after a few minutes. "You're not acting like yourself this morning. I really hope you didn't think I wouldn't notice."

Of course, you did, Kim thought to herself. "I'm cool, Mrs. Karns." Kim turned and got back to work.

Mrs. Karns is not only the school counselor, but Kim's youth Pastor and aclose friend to her mother as well. Trying to hide anything from her is pointless. "Come on, Kim, I know you all too well. Something is on your mind, and for some reason, you don't want to say. What's funny to me is that you think you're going to leave here without telling me. Well, not really funny, however, it is kind of funny, like crazy."

"I know what you mean, Mrs. Karns. It's cool," Kim said.

Kim was unsure about saying anything to Mrs. Karns for fear of betraying a friend. How many times have you desired to talk to someone, if only to bounce things off them or to get advice on how to handle a situation?

The sound of sigh after sigh and the clearing of Kim's throat ran through the room like a freight train. Mrs. Karns continued to ask what was on her mind, but unwavering Kim never even lifted her head and continued to say nothing. Picking up her pen to begin working again, Mrs. Karns decided to give it a minute and say nothing more, figuring eventually Kim would come around and open the flood gates.

After a while, Kim gave up and did just that. She began to tell Mrs. Karns that she was worried about her friend and how upset she was about what was going on. Mrs. Karns sat with a very confused look on her face, but then realized she was speaking of Tonya. There is so much that Kim does not understand. And because of her frustration with Tonya during their conversation, Kim was unable to find the root of the problem.

"I don't get it," Kim said. "I'm frustrated, and I don't know how to reach her."

"Is it really for you to figure out or is it God's to work out? A lot of times we take on the most uncontrollable things, not realizing until the last minute that only God can fix it. God can strategically put people in place that will help us see that He is in control. Let's remember we're never too far that God can't reach us."

Mrs. Karns took a deep breath and began to ask Kim questions to figure out what she thought Tonya's issue might be. "Is it peer pressure?"

"That's just it. I don't think she's being pressured. I tried to talk to her, and I completely jacked that up. She was on guard from the start, and I responded in the wrong way. She didn't want to talk, and I forced it."

"Why do you think she wanted to keep quiet?" Mrs. Karns asked.

"I'm not sure," Kim answered. "I was way too hard on her. I got upset, and I started to get back at her. She was just saying some real stupid stuff, and now she thinks I was judging her and attacking her." With a quiver in her voice, she told Mrs. Karns softly, "I didn't listen to her. If I was in her shoes, I would have wanted to be heard."

"Hmm . . . okay. Well, now you can identify this fact, you cannot react or respond in a certain way, whether with her or anyone else. That is a lesson that we all can learn. Everyone should be quick to listen, slow to speak, and slow to become angry, like it says in *James 1:19*.

It is easy to express your feelings but not so easy to stop and listen to someone else's." Mrs. Karns continued, "Answer this for me please. Is she acting out?"

"Do I think she's acting out? Well... " Kim had to stop and think for a minute how to respond to the question. "I never really saw her doing anything, but I knew it was happening and she didn't deny anything. It's crazy because I thought she was free from some things. But I don't know anymore."

"How long did it take for you to be completely delivered from things?" Mrs. Karns asked Kim.

"Well," Kim said as she put her head down.

Mrs. Karns smiled at Kim and said, "That's what I thought. Come on Kim, you know better than that. I see how this conversation, more like altercation, turned out. You are supposed to be the one to at least try to keep your cool. Had you just walked away things would be different."

"I'm human," she said, "a Christian, but at the same time, human."

"Yes, you are, that's not a good excuse, but at the same time, show others the same mercy you want shown toward you."

No matter the age, whether saved or not saved, Mrs. Karns meets you where you are. Students respect her, and parents love her because she connects with them.

"The conversation went all the way to the left." Kim sat very quietly and thought about what took place between her and Tonya. She folded her arms on the table and put her head down. Unsure how to reply, she simply said, "Okay, forget it." Kim stood up and began pacing the floor. "Yes, from my impression, she's acting out. I feel like she's doing things she shouldn't be, and I don't know how to handle that."

Mrs. Karns gave Kim the side-eye.

"I know, I know. I need to let it go. It's not for me to handle, and it's not a situation for me to have to prove."

"Did you see something that her parents should be made aware of?"

Kim just shook her head and proceeded to tell Mrs. Karns that initially Tonya would not talk to or look at her when she approached her.

"I tried talking to her later," Kim said, "and that did nothing but make us both mad. I'm pretty certain it made things worse. I'll be surprised if she talks to me again. The only thing I know to do is pray for her."

"A lot of times, Kim, all we *can* do is pray. Giving things to God is the best thing we can do, in any circumstance. You tried talking to her, now you must let go. It is not for you to try and fix. If it ended as badly as you say, approaching her again is not the right thing to do. Let her come to you. At least then you will know she wants to talk."

"I'm angry with myself because I got in the way of what God wanted to do through me. I allowed my feelings and my friendship to get in the way. I know I made it worse. No, scratch that. I didn't make it better. Meaning, I added to the chaos. I'm mad at her too because she knows the things, she is doing is wrong and yet she still continues to do them," Kim said forgetting she had been where Tonya is at that moment.

"That's like a lot of us. We struggle with things each and every day, Kim. There are days when it gets easier to let those things go and days when it gets that much harder. You are a good friend, Kim, just keep praying and asking God to tell you what to do and say. You must trust and believe that He knows what He's doing. You want to make sure you say the right things.

Be yourself but, at the same time, don't deviate from His plan, and you can't do that if you are walking in your flesh. Don't give up on her because God never gives up on you. The operative word is *you* because *you* are always messing up. You can also give her, 1 Thessalonians 5:23."

"This started somewhere," Kim said. "There has to be a reason why she's trippin'."

Mrs. Karns interrupted Kim before she continued to put her foot in her mouth. "You don't even know if she is. You cannot assume she's doing something and then turn around and call it trippin', Kim. Come on, you know better than that," she said.

"Okay, you're right," Kim said.

"I know I am," Mrs. Karns said sarcastically and laughed.

"I can't help but feel something happened to make her choose to do the types of things she is doing. I just knew God brought her out of that," Kim said as she continued to pace the floor.

"How is her home life in general, her relationship with her parents? Does she even have a relationship with her parents?" Mrs. Karns asked.

"As far as I know, everything is okay," Kim said as she sat back in her chair and shook her head. "As far as I know. But I do know that they are hardly ever home. She's clearly not telling me everything about what she is doing and going through. She's hanging out with the wrong type of people. These are people who are not thinking about God. I think it has a lot to do with them. No, I know it has a lot to do with them. They are not helping her."

Mrs. Karns said, "You could be right. The devil does use anything and anyone to do his bidding, but again, you are speculating. However, let me say this. Just because people do not choose the straight path does not mean they are not thinking about God. You must also understand you teach people how to treat you and interact with you."

"I know, but she kicks it with them on a regular, before, after, and even during school. They are not good or healthy for her, naturally or spiritually. There are times when we are supposed to hang out, and she'll call me and tell me that she can't do it. Last night she was supposed to write a paper for class, and I was told that she was doing other things. And it didn't sound good at all. Just thinking about it is driving me crazy."

"Are you mad about that? You are not her only friend Kim. Let me also add, no one is perfect, Kim. Let's remember that we all struggle with things. Don't forget that and be careful that you are not judging her, or anyone else for that matter." Mrs. Karns paused for a moment but decided to continue. "I don't understand why you feel responsible for her. You can only do so much, just like God can only do what we allow Him to do for us. She has a choice to serve God or the devil."

Wanting nothing more than to make Kim feel secure in the fact that she is a good friend, Mrs. Karns walked over and sat down beside her. "Look, Kim, we must allow the Lord to do a work in our lives. God is not going to force Himself on our friends, no more than He did you and me. I know you love her like a sister, and I know it hurts to see someone you know, and love fall and struggle to get back up. It may take something drastic to make her see, like it does for a lot of us. However, you must remember that God has it all under control. You must let go of the control because it is not for you to carry. Keep praying for her and then stand back and watch God work. Well, the bell is going to ring soon. You can finish your work another day.

Make sure you continue praying for her and asking God to give you guidance on what to do and say. Don't forget that we serve an almighty God. There is nothing He cannot do."

As she turned to grab her things, Kim said, "Thank you, Mrs. Karns. This really helped me. I was a little jacked up when I got here. I don't know what I would do if you were not here. There's nothing like having another Believer to talk to at school."

"Come see me before you leave school today if you need to talk."

"I will. Thanks again, Mrs. Karns," Kim said while hugging her before walking out the door.

No one wants to have a friendship or relationship that seems hopeless and full of regret at the same time. Kim wondered if she would even have the opportunity to implement anything, considering Tonya no longer wanted to speak.

CHAPTER SUMMARY

We must admit, some of our friends and acquaintances have an eccentric way of expressing themselves, and at any given moment, as well. I know all too well, there is a time to listen and a time to turn a deaf ear. We have the tendency to push people away and feel the need to put up walls to protect ourselves from those same people. You know what those walls represent? They represent protection from feelings of guilt, hurt, being used, abused, at the same time being rejected.

There have been so many situations I felt, turned my life upside down. With nowhere to turn, I continued to stay strong for appearance's sake. Nothing and no one could help me from what I knew. Do not think that just because you see someone who looks nice, carries a nice bag, and wears nice shoes that they have not a care in the world. You can have the finest whip and still be unhappy. You can have all the money needed to survive and then some and still have no peace. Stop and think about it. What else will make all things better?

Let go of the fact that you are alone. Forget about the notion that you cannot be forgiven. I have said it once and I'll say it again, you can *never* do anything that will make God cease to show you love. Your life has been predestined, well before it began. Don't you think He can control every situation?

God knows all and He sees all. He knows each and every one of us by name. He knows who tries and who does not. He knows your needs before you do. Who are we as a people to judge ourselves, let alone another individual? Stop thinking t h a t you a r e not good enough and you cannot succeed. You have the power within you to move mountains because your Heavenly Father says so.

Listen, this is funny to me. There are people who take credit from God, whether intentionally or not. There are people who jump in the ring and take on a fight that is not their own nor can they win. Credit is taken away from the person it belongs to. I am guilty of that very thing. There are people who have the right intentions but, like a pit bull, cannot release their grip of control.

It is hard to give everything over to God, no matter how big or small. Literally, opening your hand and giving someone the opportunity to take it away is not always an easy thing to do.

Life is about priorities, making choices, and deciding what and who is most important in your life. It is difficult from time to time, for our youth to do this alone. Some need guidance. Who is going to affect positive change in their lives? Do not just sit back and criticize them and their parents. Our youth may be in a situation where their parents are not present. Some may have a little more freedom to act out or get into trouble, than others. Simply put, it is hard for some of our youth to decide between right and wrong.

The key is to let go and get out of your own way and let God help you, no matter your age. But who is going to assist in showing them the right way, if all we do is sit back and criticize?

Every so often, it is not someone else blocking our way, it is us, the individual. We are the wall that is keeping us from getting to the other side. Our own thoughts are the stumbling block, the deciding factor between right and wrong.

We as adults cannot get it right from time to time, so how can we expect our youth to do the same. We as adults and society can put a tremendous amount of pressure on our youth.

Let go of your will and give it to God so He can change your life. Not believing that God can change you, can fix you, and repair what has been broken in you can prevent you from experiencing all of the things that have been predestined for you. The power of the love of God is astonishing. We must choose to let go and give God the control.

CHAPTER SIX

Kim turned the corner, and in the blink of an eye she felt a sense of urgency. There she was, the young lady who affected Kim in such a way, even she could not explain. Kim could feel the beat of her heart in her throat. Smaller and smaller the room became by the minute. She stopped and contemplated turning around and walking the other way. After swallowing the lump in her throat, she got herself together and tried to remember everything she discussed with Mrs. Karns. Kim decided to let whatever happens, happen. She turned around and proceeded to walk down the hallway, but the closer Tonya gets, the more Kim thought it was a stupid idea. Possibly having to confront a friend about a problem makes Kim want to vomit.

It is what it is, Kim said to herself.

The look on Tonya's face was strangely cold. She put her books in her locker and motioned for Kim to come over to her.

"Hey girl, I'm really sorry about yesterday. I don't know what I was thinking, but I know how I felt. I felt attacked right off the rip, and because of that I wasn't trying to hear what you had to say. Real talk. For some reason, you had this crazy picture of me in your head, assuming things without even asking me first," Tonya said.

"It's cool. Don't worry about it. Just don't let it happen again," Kim said sarcastically.

Tonya was unsure if Kim was serious or if she was playing and did not know how to respond.

"Okay Goliath, giants fall hard. Do you really think you want to go there with me?" Tonya said taking a step forward.

Kim looked at Tonya and said firmly, "I'm just playin' David, dang. No need to be all serious. I didn't mean for you to feel attacked at all. That was not my intention."

"Well," Tonya said, "I thought about it, and I didn't think it was cool for me to come at you the way I did, either. You're my best friend..." She said, with much regret in her voice. "I shouldn't have let myself get that mad. I just want to let you know I heard you. I'm just so stressed out, and I've got alot of things on my mind. I'm not sure how to deal with everything I'm going through."

Kim made sure Tonya knew she was not alone and that their friendship meant a great deal to her. Kim realized in that instant that Tonya needed a listening ear and nothing more. A friend loves at all times. Friendship is a bond that is created by two people. It is as good or as bad as each person makes it. We must always be slow to speak and quick to listen, in any given situation.

"I'll do that," Tonya said quietly looking down at the floor. "I think we both need to work on our friendship skills though. For real, I really appreciate it. When—"

Before Tonya could get out what she needed to say, Jeff walked up and interrupted her. "What's up cutie?" he said in a loud and obnoxious tone.

He threw his arm around Kim and tried to walk her away from Tonya. No way Tonya was going to let Jeff off easy.

"More than you know," Tonya said while giving Jeff a look that could kill. It is clear that neither of them is fond of the other.

"Tonya, that wasn't meant for you,"Jeff said as he rolled his eyes and stepped in between Kim and Tonya.

"I could care less what you say is or is not for me. You ain't nobody," Tonya said as nasty as she could.

"Don't you have somewhere to be, anyway?" Jeff asked. "You need to go there. I need to talk to Kim for a minute." He looked at Tonya from head to toe, threw his hand in her face, and turned to continue talking to Kim.

"Jeff you can't be serious!" Tonya yelled. "We were talking."

Tonya was so upset she slammed her hand down on Jeff's shoulder and turned him completely around.

Tonya pushed Jeff off of Kim and yelled, "Go away!"

"Dang you two are like oil and water. What the mess? Not right now, Jeff," Kim said. "Please, I'm talking to Tonya right now."

"We were talking, and I hate to break it to you, Jeff, it's not about you," Tonya said. "You see this is a daily thing. Kim, he just doesn't know when to quit. You're wasting your time, Jeff, go away!"

"Tonya, once again, I am not talking to you, and you're just dying inside about that aren't you? That's why you're always barking when I try to talk to Kim. It's not healthy for you to be a jealous person."

"Okay you guys, that's enough." Kim said while pulling them apart. "Not now, Jeff, and Tonya's right. You are wasting your time. You're not my type and you try too hard. You wouldn't annoy people if you didn't try so hard. It's very irritating."

Kim tried to bring the volume down because people were beginning to stare. Jeff stood in disbelief that Kim was not interested in him. The look on Jeff's face was tragic. No longer would he accept that Kim was not his type. He stood quiet for a minute, and leaned up against the locker. He tried to understand why nothing he did worked with Kim, and why he was unable to get her attention. No matter what he did, Kim was not going to budge. The more he approached her, the more he pushed her away. He began to think that Tonya was thereason why Kim was not interested in him, which made him very upset.

"You have two point two seconds to get out of my face, Tonya," Jeff muttered.

"What was that Jeff?" Tonya said as she put her hand up to her ear, as if to say, "I didn't hear you."

Jeff decided to say nothing to Tonya. Kim watched the two of them go at it in amazement.

Tonya asked again in a nasty tone, "What did you say, Jeff?" Tonya snarled at Jeff, using sign language to get his attention.

"Why don't you go somewhere, Tonya? The class is held inside the classroom. You know what you should do?"

"I can't bring myself to like you. Jeff, as a person or man's best friend," Tonya said. "Everything you do makes my skin crawl."

"Go in the classroom and sit boo boo, sit," Jeff said as he pointed inside the room. "Have a seat."

Kim jumped in between Jeff and Tonya, grabbed Tonya's arm to keep her from punching Jeff.

"Jeff, Tonya, you two need to stop. This is crazy man, and I'm not tryin' to hear it." Kim said. "Stop it!" She said to Jeff. "You see what we're saying? You were about to get hit, Jeff. You just don't know when enough is enough."

Jeff could not believe Kim was saying something to him about how he was acting, when to him, Tonya was acting just as bad.

"You're getting on me, but she's acting foul too. Really, Kim, you can't see that she's trippin'?" He asked.

"Jeff, oh my goodness! You know I don't like calling people stupid, but man, you are really acting stupid right now. I mean really!" Kim said throwing her hands up.

Not willing to accept defeat, Jeff began attacking Tonya, "What's your type, Tonya? The devil?" Not giving Tonya a chance to answer the question, Jeff said, "Must be 'cause you're hanging out with Tim of all people."

"Leave Tim out of this," Tonya yelled. "If that were true that would mean I liked you and that is so far from the truth. Do you hear yourself when you speak?" She said as she chuckled. "You are a hot mess. See, Kim, that's what I'm talking about."

"All of these questions are directed toward Kim," Jeff said trying to be mean, "but, yet you keep answering them. Why is that Tonya?"

"I don't want my friend to be subjected to stupidity, that's why," Tonya said.

"Why not, she puts up with your mess every day," Jeff said trying to be funny.

Jeff threw up his hand in Tonya's face and turned to look at Kim.

"Go the heck away," she screamed. "And save yourself the embarrassment, Jeff. Kim, I'll be back in a minute. I can't take any more of this." Tonya rolled her eyes and jumped at Jeff like she wanted to hit him, before walking away. "Get rid of him, please."

"Hurry up, the bell is about to ring." Kim shakes her head at Jeff. "You two are something else."

As you can see, Tonya and Jeff are not each other's fan. Kim always finds herself jumping in between the two of them and sending them to their respective corners. Neither found it necessary to get along, not even for Kim's sake. I'm sure you have friends that act this way. We should not allow anyone to take us outside of who we are. It is very much like being in a boxing ring with Tonya and Jeff.

Kim and Jeff began to walk toward the Study Hall. The entire time Kim wished Jeff would just give up and walk away. *That would be too much like right*, Kim thought to herself.

There is something to say for Jeff's persistence. No matter what, he will not let go of the fact that he has feelings for Kim. He believes that if he presses her enough, she will give in.

Not thinking that she would either hit him, not speak to him anymore, or both. Once they arrived, they walked in and took their seats. Jeff continued to talk to Kim about getting to know her and why she would not allow that to happen. Not realizing that bugging her was one reason why. This he would soon find out.

"Okay class, if you don't have any work to do that is fine, but let's make it our business to talk quietly," the instructor stressed. "If not, you're going to give me business, and neither one of us wants that. Do not disturb those who have work to do. You know, have some business, you feel me? If there are any questions, please come up to see me."

"Kim, why are you so mean to me? You act like you don't like me. What's up with that?" Jeff asked.

With a confused look on her face, Kim said, "Wow, you really don't get it do you? Jeff, it's not that I don't like you," she said without looking at him, "you just get on my nerves."

"Oh, like that's better," Jeff said as he rolled his eyes.

"You pick the wrong times to annoy me. One of the things about being a man is having the wisdom to know what to do."

"Jeff and Kim get some business," the teacher said. "This is not communication class."

Picking up where he left off, Jeff said, "Look Kim, I just—"

Kim looked up and asked God as she laughed. "Why are You doing this to me?" "What are you talking about?" Kim asked Jeff. "Just what? Look, I don't dislike you at all. You do drive me crazy though. You don't know when to quit, Jeff. Like you're doing right now, and you don't know how to keep your hands to yourself."

"Like this morning?" He asked with a sincere tone.

"Jeff, like right now. Get your hand off my knee, and yes, this morning is another example. You don't respect me sometimes, and that's not cool with me. Please understand that I am saved and there are things that I expect and do not accept. I expect not to be touched and to be treated a certain way, and I will not accept anything less. Don't get it twisted. You are a nice guy *at times*, but you don't give people a chance to see that nice guy because after a few seconds of being in a room with you, they end up wanting to leave."

"Wow, that's deep. I didn't know I had that effect on you," he said jokingly.

Jeff thought that was really funny, but the look that Kim gave him was proof the sentiments were not the same. It took everything for Kim not to get up and walk out of Study Hall. However, that would not be good *business* for Kim.

"See, that's what I'm saying. Why don't you take things seriously? Nobody will ever take you *seriously* because you play too dag-on much, Jeff. You drive me nuts. Like, you make me feel like I'm going insane. I want to go running through the hallway screaming at the top of my lungs right now. Like, for real."

Finally, Jeff is beginning to understand, "Sorry, Kim. Dang, calm down," he muttered. Sitting back in his seat and put his head down, saying absolutely nothing. Then here it comes.

"Isn't your father the pastor of that church on the corner of Smith and Watkins?" Kim asked.

"Yeah, he is," Jeff answered. "You on one right now, man. I know where this is going. Yeah, yeah, he is."

"So, what's—"

Before Kim could even ask the question, Jeff cut her off.

"Nah, never mind," he stood up and said. "I don't want to hear it!"

Jeff has tried with everything in him to run from the fact that his father is a pastor. He wants nothing more than to be 'his own person' and to run from the call on his life.

The instructor questioned, "Jeff, what are you thinking about? You look real good sitting down!"

"Yeah, sit down," Kim added.

"I do not need your assistance Kim, trust me. You are supposed to be studying. I know you of all people got some business, get to it. Do I need to separate the two of you like children?"

As he sat back down in his seat, Jeff said, "Let me school you on something, Ms. Kimberly. Not all preachers' kids like to be defined by their parents. They want to find their own way, not be forced to live life through them or be identified by them."

Ignoring his defensive tone, Kim said, "Jeff, this is the impression I get from you, ministry and Christianity are not as important to you. Having and pleasing your friends are of more value. If you don't want people to think a certain way about you, show them something different."

"What are you trying to say, Kim? Don't act like you know me. You never take the time to get to know who I am.

You've said that in so many words. Yes, I like to go out and hang with my friends. No, I don't drink or smoke. I do not do any of the crazy things that my friends do, but you know—"

"No, I don't know," Kim stressed. "You are to be set apart from all that mess. The Lord said you are to keep away from anything that might take God's place in your heart. What scripture is that, um." Kim stopped to think. "*First John 5:21*. It seems to me that hanging out with your friends is more important to you than doing what God wants you to do."

"Yeah, whatever," Jeff said. As he shifted in his seat and folded his arms with an attitude. "I know all of that, Kim. I give up," he said.

"Now you gonna sit there and pout like somebody done stole your bike. What's the problem? You can't handle the truth?" Kim asked. "I'm sorry, but I have no sympathy for those who know and won't do."

"I choose to keep the friends I have. I see nothing wrong with that. Don't look at me like that. I love God, and He knows I do. I know how to balance my friendships and my walk with God. You're trippin'," Jeff said emphatically.

"I'm looking at you that way because you make no sense to me. How can you say you know how to balance your friendships with your walk with God? When are you going to be all in with God? I believe and this is only my opinion, don't get mad at me and make excuses about why you don't want to obey God. It's your choice. We both know you have not totally surrendered," Kim said.

Kim continued to hit the right buttons. The more she said, the more furious Jeff became. "Yeah, my choice, so why are you on my case about it?" Jeff stressed.

"How can you say I am on your case, Jeff? Are you for real? You're funny to me. You should be making better choices in what you think about and the way you spend your time. I go out and kick it with my friends all the time and we enjoy our time out. But there are people that I had to let go because I found myself slipping when I was out with them. Talking on the phone with them had me thinking bad thoughts. I had to let them loose. They weren't good for me, and you should be mature enough spiritually to make that decision as well. I love myself too much. I didn't do it just for myself though. I did it for God too. I refuse to crucify Him again. I choose to serve God and not entertain the devil."

Jeff responded, "I'm glad you think you have all the answers, and you do no wrong. You do you and I'll do me. It's not that simple for me, Kim."

"And why not?" Kim said in a sarcastic tone. "I am so mad at you right now. No one said serving God was easy. There are several things that try to knock us off track. That is why we have the Holy Spirit and the word to help us not be affected. I am not saying anything you don't already know. Maybe that's why you're getting so irate."

"I mean what? These are my friends that I've had for a long time. They know that I am a PK, and they don't test that."

"But you can?" Kim said. "They don't have to because you're doing it for them. You are compromising, and how is that okay? Ask God what He thinks about what you are doing. What do you think He will say? I don't think He is very happy about the choices you are making."

"Who do you think you are? So, *you* think you're better than me? You don't know what's best for me."

"I know what God said, and I know what He has in store if we do what He said. Wow—" Kim hated the expression Jeff had on his face. "Let's welcome the I don't care attitude now, why don't we," Kim stated.

"Yeah well," Jeff said.

"Is that your answer for everything, Jeff?" Throwing her hand up as if she is completely fed up with Jeff. "Yeah well—ridiculous."

"You're still no better than me," Jeff responded.

"What is that supposed to mean? You know what, I'm not even going to entertain that. I'm not judging you at all because I've been where you are."

"Exactly!" Jeff said interrupting Kim.

"I've been where you haven't, and God delivered me. It was hard for me too, but God brought me out. I had to end those past relationships and stop hanging out with those people because my soul was more important to me. They understood because I gave them no other choice. Besides," Kim continued to say as she gathered her things, "they knew how much God meant to me. You need to do the same, and guess what? If they do not understand, oh well. Your soul should be more important to you, too. Excuse me."

CHAPTER SUMMARY

Grasp this, balance is not about making your friends the focus and balancing everything else around them. Do you think God would want someone to be equal to or weigh more in your life than Him? God does not want to be compared to anything or anyone. Nor does He want anyone to take higher precedence in your life. Just as quickly as something is given to you, it can be taken away, simply because you put it before God. You are straddling making things idols when doing so. Idolatry begins when we lose sight of Jesus. Consider this scripture:

"You shall not make for yourself a carved image—any likeness of anything that is in heaven above, or that is in the earth beneath, or that is in the water under the earth; you shall not bow down to them nor serve them. For I, the LORD your God, am a jealous God, visiting the iniquity of the fathers upon the children to the third and fourth generations of those who hate

Me, but showing mercy to thousands, to those who love Me and keep My commandments."
    Exodus 20:4-6 NKJV

Ungodly relationships can become idols. If a relationship pulls you away from God, causes you to do things that are not of God, it will not be blessed, it will not prosper, it will not grow but wither away. This can also be the same for friendships.

We know that God places certain people in our lives for many reasons. How often do you think about why you were friends with someone or dated a person? I know I have quite often. It could be for you or the other individual, and even for just a little while, maybe not for a lifetime. Still, it does not afford you the right to live an ungodly lifestyle. I am a firm believer that everything happens for a reason. Everyone who has the privilege of being in your life has influenced you, be it positive or negative. Keep in mind, like Jeff, most people never mean to annoy you or want to make a negative impact on your life. You must also understand the way you respond is equally important.

This is for the parents: As parents, we tend to forget that our teens deal with their own set of issues. Issues such as peer pressure, domestic violence, broken homes, drug, and alcohol abuse run rampant in some families across this Nation. Several teens are easily influenced with no chance of survival. Yes, it is hard for our younger generation when there is a plethora of things that are not of God to get into. Therefore, it is important for us as adults to help steer them in the right direction, and we cannot do that without God. Trust and believe that not only is it hard for those who do not know God, but it is equally as hard for those who do.

Jeff is a prime example of allowing the things of this world to come in between his relationship with God. It is difficult to not yield to temptation and to walk away from certain aspects of the world. Consider this also.

"We all experience times of testing, which is normal for every human being. But God will be faithful to you. He will screen and filter the severity, nature, and timing of every test or trial you face so that you can bear it.

And each test is an opportunity to trust him more, for along with every trial God has provided for you a way of escape that will bring you out of it victoriously. My cherished friends, keep on running far away from idolatry. I know I am writing to thoughtful people, so carefully consider what I say."

1 Corinthians 10:13-15 TPT

The devil wraps our temptations in the most attractive packages at times. When friends make it look so pleasurable to do the wrong things, keep in mind that God wants us to bear His image and likeness, not take on the actions and likeness of our friends. We are not to copy the things of the world, but the things of our Heavenly Father.

We must choose to either serve God or the devil. We must choose to be all in on one type of lifestyle. We cannot live for God and do things that are not of God.

CHAPTER SEVEN

Our hearts and our minds struggle just to get through the day. We ask ourselves questions like; How can I be filled with so much pain but feel so empty? How can I know where I am but be lost at the same time? When is someone going to love and care for me? These are questions that Tonya asks herself every day. Not having anyone she can trust is a problem for her. Tonya feels no one will listen, try to understand, and not judge her. It is hard for Tonya to hold it inside. It hurts all over. Consequently, she finds the remedy for it all. Tonya is fighting against a very strong force, and she's weak.

Tonya continued walking through the halls. Whenever she heard someone coming, she would hide in the bathroom or an empty classroom.

I do not want to be in school today. I wish I had a car so I could leave, she thought to herself. *I have so many scars, and they are so deep. They may not be physical scars that you can see.*

There's such an enormous amount of pain that there's no room for joy, peace, or God. I want You, Lord. I know that I need You, but— there is a constant reminder of just how lost I am every time I go home. I'm forced to be alone and made to feel as though every bad thing in my life is my fault, and never praised for the good that I do. I just want to know that I'm loved. Why must I keep taking the blame for their mistakes? I'm getting it from all sides, my heart, my mind, my friends, and family, even me. How do I get through this? It's hard when I'm always pushed aside like none of my cares matter much. It's always about the next person. What about me? I try to love and care about everyone else, but what about me? Who is going to be there for me? Who and when? That's what I want to know. I'm comin' to You as real as I know how, man. Isn't that what You want me to do? Save me, please. I know You did once on the cross, that time in the car, I guess that would be twice. Wow, and in countless relationships. Yep, so many times. I need to be saved again. I'm not gonna lie.

Leah ran up behind Tonya and put her arms around her, "Girl, are you talking to yourself? Don't do that. You look crazy. What are you doing in the hall anyway?Don't you have class this period?"

"Wassup, Leah. I have Study Hall, but I'm really not trying to be there right now. I need to get going though, before I get in trouble."

"You don't have to go do you? You shouldn't go. Come with us."

Knowing that leaving would not be a good thing, Tonya shook her head. "I don't know. I don't want to go to class, but like I said I'm not trying to get in trouble either. I ain't got that to do."

"Where are you going anyway?" she asked.

"Tim and I are going to the mall to eat," Leah said. "I want you to come with us, Tonya."

"I don't know. I think I should just stay here, for real," Tonya said. "Go ahead, handle your business."

Tonya knew that leaving would be a bad thing to do. She knows some of the things Leah is into. At the same time, Tonya does not know everything. Keep in mind, everything happens for a reason; good or bad.

"No, I'm good. You two go ahead. I'll catch up with you when you get back." Tonya said.

Leah had her mind dead set on getting Tonya to go, so she grabbed Tonya's arm to keep her from walking away. "I don't want to go with Tim by myself," Leah said as she pouted. "I got some smoke left, even though I know you don't really smoke. Come on go with us. You know good and well you don't want to be here. Keep it real with ya' girl, you know you don't. Let's hangout."

"All right, dang! Let me put my stuff in my locker and run to the bathroom. I'll be right back," Tonya said as she headed down the hall.

"Leah, come on, let's go," Tim yelled.

"Here I come Tim. Don't rush me and don't be walkin' up on me like you crazy. You better be glad you my boy. You feel me?" Leah said.

"You know we got stuff to do. I'm driving, and if you're rollin' with me, you better come on or you can walk. It's up to you," Tim said.

Tim and Leah are very close friends, close enough that they say they are brother and sister. They are not your ordinary students, as they have a past and quite a bit to hide. Things will be explained shortly.

"Hey, man, I got Tonya to hang with us," Leah whispered quietly in Tim's ear.

Leah wanted to make sure Tonya was not coming down the hall. She feared Tonya walking up and hearing what they were talking about.

"What were you thinkin'? I'm trying to hit me some stores, not babysit. Not to mention, I don't need her knowing my business," Tim shouted.

Tim pushed Leah away from him and started pacing the floor. The whole time Leah is wondering why he is reacting the way he is. She put her foot up on the lockers, leaned back, and watched the performance.

"Tim quit trippin'. I told her we were going to the mall to eat. She doesn't know what we're doing. She can help us though," Leah said. "You are buggin' out for absolutely no reason and for what. Dang!"

"No, you're trippin'. How do you think she can do that?" Tim asked Leah.

"What is wrong with you? It's not that serious, man. It's just the mall. Dang, you need to breathe dude. Sit down. Think about it. She can actually buy, while we're not," Leah explained.

Tim began to get very frustrated even more because he wanted to make sure Tonya had nothing to do with that part of his life. There were certain things he would do when Tonya was around.

Tim knew there were rumors around school about him, but he wanted to leave it as that, rumors.

"Whatever, Leah, let's go. I don't understand why you would put her into what we got goin' on. That makes absolutely no sense to me."

"Shh, here she comes," Leah told to Tim. "That was quick, Tonya."

"Leah, you finally ready to go?" Tim said turning his back to Tonya. "Where we wanna go first?"

"I know you did not just turn your back on me like that," Tonya said surprised by what just happened. "Why are you acting like I'm not standing here, Tim? What do you mean where you wanna go first? I thought we were going to the mall to eat?"

"Hi Tonya," he said mockingly. "Would you like to run through somewhere and get something to eat first and then we can go to the mall?"

"You know what—" Tonya threw her hand up and started to walk away. "Leah, I'm not going. I refuse to put up with his crap today. Talkin' to me like that, I'm not gonna do." She turned to Tim and pointed. "Nah, wait. Why are you trying to pick a fight with me, Tim?" she asked walking toward Tim.

"I can't believe I ever—"

Tim stopped talking before he said something to Tonya he would regret later. The entire time Leah is standing there, watching this display from her friends, both looking very suspect.

"Ever what, Tim? Hmm, what were you going to say?" Tonya put her finger in his face. "You're going a bit too far today. Trust me when I say this is not the day you want to mess with me. Cut it out."

Tonya turned to walk away, and Leah threw her hands up as if to say, "What about me?"

"Why *you* actin' funny, Tonya?" Tim asked.

Tonya stopped, paused for a second, and turned around. She began to count to ten and was unsuccessful in calming down. She quickly walked to Tim and dealt with the issue. Tim backed up from Tonya because he knew she was serious. Tonya could not understand why Tim was being so mean to her.

"Why am I acting funny? No, why are you acting funny, Tim? I don't understand. Why are you talking to me like this, and why are you changing plans? The only reason I was going in the first place was to eat and then you're bringin' me back here!"

Tim replied, "You ain't gotta go. You can stay right here!"

"Tim, stop it," Leah said. "Tonya is my friend, and I want her to go. What's up with you two? Why are ya'll gettin' at each other like this? Is something going on I don't know about?"

Tonya shot Tim with a confused look and yelled, "Whatever, man, we can just eat at the food court in the mall like it was decided in the beginning. I'm ready to go," Tonya said.

Tonya began to think either she is extra sensitive, or Tim is beginning to feel differently about her. He has always been the one she could count on, gentle and attentive. Now, out of the blue he is treating her bad. There are always things about our friends that we may not know.

What is he trying to hide? Is he ashamed of me? Tonya thought to herself.

We cannot allow the things that people say or do define who we are. I cannot stress enough; we should not allow them to take us outside of who we are as a person or Christian.

"Tonya, you ready? Come on. Let's go," Leah said.

While they were on their way out the door, Tim's phone rang. When he saw who it was, he decided to take the call away from the girls and told them to meet him outside by the car. The type of friend you cannot bring home to mom is on the other end of the phone, and she is an acquaintance of Tim's. That should tell you something. Nika, the individual who supplies him with the product to sell, is the type of person you wish you would never have to come in contact with. Yes, she is a female, and yes, Tim works for her, making drops around town. Although he's never been caught, he constantly thinks about the day when his luck will run out.

Nika is very adamant about Tim coming to her house and making a drop for her right now. Back and forth, Tim tried to explain to Nika that he does not like to make runs during school hours. His education is very important to him. However, making money to give to his mother is more important. Nevertheless, crossing Nika is not something he wants to do either.

"Nika, you know I can't do anything during the day," Tim stressed to her. "I just told you I got school. It will have to wait 'til later."

"What time is later?" Nika was not going to let up on Tim. She has her own agenda for him. "You let me know what time you wanna roll out here to make this money, since I'm working on your time schedule now," she said sarcastically.

"It would have to be after school, Nika. I. Am. At. School," Tim yelled.

"I'm gonna need you to lower your voice," Nika said.

It takes a lot to make Tim angry, and Nika knows just what buttons to push. Tim and Nika have been what you would call associates for a while at that point. For about six months, Tim has been pulled in two directions. Torn between Tonya and his life in the streets, and whether to stop or continue. Stop hustling and continue to see Tonya or continue with his life in the streets.

"Nah, man, you fail to realize I have school during the day. I may be getting lunch, but I have to come back here."

As demanding as she could be, Nika said, "I know what time you get out of school Tim. So do not make me come out there to look for you. You know I have a right mind to tell someone else to do this job.

But I'm trying to do you a favor because you're broke. Bet I won't no more. Time is money, and I need to make my money. You know what I'm sayin'? If you can't do it later, let me know right now, and I'll hit up somebody else."

"I said I'd be there after school. Besides, you haven't paid me for the last run I made for you."

Hoping the conversation was ending, Tim began making his way out of the building. Trying to avoid running into teachers, he went out the back door of the school and walked around to student parking.

"I'll pay you for that when I give you the money for this job. It doesn't sound like you at school anyway," Nika said.

"I'm outside now, and it's my lunch period. I'm going to get some lunch at the mall with friends and then we're comin' back to school."

Selfishly, Nika asked, "You can't come by here before you go to the mall? You're leaving school anyway."

"Bro, for the last time, my friends are with me. I'm not trying to come out there with them in the car. And I'm not trying to get kicked out of school either."

"Who is it? Leah? You make runs with her all the time. Look, it's really simple, there are people waitin' for this product, and I don't wanna keep them waitin' long." With a cynical tone, Nika added, "There's really no need for you to go to the mall anyway because you ain't got no money."

"How do you know what I got? You don't know what's in my pockets. You really trippin' right now, man."

Afraid of running into teachers in the parking lot, Tonya and Leah began walking to the car to meet Tim. Neither of them was prepared to suffer the consequences if they were caught.

"Leah, where is he at?" Tonya asked. "I am really not trying to get hemmed up today. Why didn't we just wait inside for him?"

"I have no idea where he is, girl. I'm with you," Leah said. "Girl, you know these teachers be acting like the parking lot police at this school. They are worse than flashlight cops for real," Leah said. "We should have waited in the school."

"Here he comes. Dang, is he's still on the phone? Nobody has that much to say," Tonya said in a suspicious way. "I want to know who he's talking to."

Not too happy with Tim, Leah laid into him. "Come on, Tim, we are ready to go. You are the slowest person I know. Dang, boy, why are you still on the phone? Who are you talking to, Tim? Tell them bye and come on."

Tim waved Leah off to get her to stop talking. "Hold on a minute, Nika. Leah, you see me on the phone, quit trippin', and wait a minute before I knock you out."

"Who do you think you talking to though? Because I know you ain't talking to me like that," Leah said.

Leah stepped back and folded her arms, disgusted at Tim.

"You better get outta here with all that nonsense before you get beat down by a girl," Leah said with an attitude.

"Why is it that you need me to come right now? Why can't it wait?" Tim throws his hand up to get Leah to be quiet. "Walk away, Leah," he shouted.

"Don't be wavin' me off, Tim! I want to know why you are about to tell me we're not going?" Leah said.

Nika was relentless about getting Tim over there, and Leah is on the other ear yelling at him, as well. The longer the conversation continued, the more suspicious Tonya became, and Tim knew he would have to deal with her later.

Leah's growing agitation and Nika's persistence, the more Tim wanted to say the heck with everyone. Nika was well aware that he needed the money and refused to wait until he got out of school. Eventually Tim gave in and decided to go and make the run for Nika. Not wanting to deal with Leah and Tonya, Tim proceeded to just get in his car and leave without saying a word to Leah and Tonya both.

Leah stood in the middle of the parking lot dumb founded at what just took place. As she turned to watch Tim drive away, she received a text message from him.

"Are you serious?" Leah yelled to Tonya. "He really just hopped in his car and took off without saying a word." She stood with a stunned look on her face. "I really want to slap his face right now. You feel me?"

Tonya, completely clueless about everything, said, "I want to know what's goin' on. I thought we were going to the mall. How's he just gonna blow me off?" Tonya interjected.

"What did you say?" Leah asked.

"Nothin'. I'm talking to myself. Why do you think he would leave like that?"

"How's he gonna do *me* like that?" Leah said.

"That's what I—"

Shaking her head at Tonya, "Rhetorical. Wasn't really askin'," Leah quickly stated. "I just really want to throw a temper- tantrum right now." Leah said as she laughed. "This is some crazy mess right here."

"Why am I dealing with these three crazy females," Tim said as he pulled off, "and I'm about to do somethin' I don't want to do. I have to chill out for real. This is the last time."

Things have got to change in Tim's life. He knows he cannot continue to run drugs and put himself in harm's way any longer. But we don't always do what we know to do.

After quickly parking, Tim took his hands off the wheel, hesitantly opened the door and stepped out of the car. He stood there for a moment with his hand on the top of the car. His heart beating faster and faster with each step he took. Slowly, he headed up the walkway, saying to himself, *Last time. Last time.* He grabbed his chest, wondering why he was so nervous as if he'd never done this before. "Come on, man," Tim told himself. This time felt different, his heart told him it wasn't the same.

This is where the music in the movie would get louder and more suspenseful and you are yelling at the television, *turn around, dummy, get back in the car! ARE YOU CRAZY?* He walked up to the door and knocked.

Now, you are sitting on the edge of your seat saying, *that was just stupid. Should have gotten back in the car.* And you are wondering what is going to happen next. The door opens and Tim is pulled in without warning.

CHAPTER SUMMARY

Tonya was clear in her decision not to leave school for fear of getting into trouble, however she did not stand firm on that decision. Leah remained consistent in swaying Tonya and persistent in helping her do the wrong thing.

Stand firm on our promise to God and to ourselves that we will be consistent in our walk and in our talk. Remember God is faithful; we too must remain faithful. Regardless of the fact that cutting school is the wrong thing to do, Tonya and Leah made up in their minds that they were going to do so anyway.

Tim was tired of running, but how tired was he? He reached his destination, and he hesitated to get out of the car. Knowing he no longer wanted to live his life the way he was, the hesitation did not deter him from going. He allowed the problems of the world to drive him, and the desire to live a better life could not influence him. His belief was that it is fast money, not realizing it will not last.

Simply because his options at the end of the day are prison or death, the deciding factor is Tim. Almost deciding not to get out of the car and to go back to school, the pull of the devil was stronger than the voice of the Lord inside him. There was a tug of war going on in the atmosphere, with the angels on one side and the demons on the other. This is why the deciding factor is Tim. Who would he give in to, the call of the Lord or the pull of the devil? When will enough be enough? Not only does God put people in place to help us, He speaks to us to help us along the way.

When we begin to feel like we are walking through fire, and it is always one thing after another, be still and listen. Talk to The Lord, He does not bite, He loves you. When life gets harder and everything around you begin to shake, remember the three Rs: Relax, Relate, and Release. *Relax...* Consider this scripture:

"Jesus replied, "Loving me empowers you to obey my word. And my Father will love you so deeply that we will come to you and make you our dwelling place. But those who don't love me will not obey my words. The Father did not send me to speak my own revelation, but the words of my Father. I am telling you this while I am still with you. But when the Father sends the Spirit of

Holiness, the One like me who sets you free, he will teach you all things in my name. And he will inspire you to remember every word that I've told you. "I leave the gift of peace with you—my peace. Not the kind of fragile peace given by the world, but my perfect peace. Don't yield to fear orbe troubled in your hearts—instead, be courageous!"

John 14:23-27 TPT

Be still and know He is God, and He has got your back. Give everything to Him, no matter how big or small. In Exodus 33:14 The Lord told Moses *I will give you rest—everything will be fine for you.* We must stand on that and know God will not leave you to deal with your issues alone. You do not have to suffer in secret. Lay back and relax. Let him be your peace and find rest in Him.

Another way to find peace is to read the bible. There are things in the word, comfort in the word that you cannot find in the world. Before you pick up your bible, pray and ask The Lord to reveal to you what you need so that you can begin to relax. Everything you need, things you can apply to your life is right there for you. *Relate...*

If you need peace.

"Be cheerful with joyous celebration in every season of life. Let joy overflow, for you are united with the Anointed One! Let gentleness be seen in every relationship, for our Lord is ever near. Don't be pulled in different directions or worried about a thing. Be saturated in prayer throughout each day, offering your faith-filled requests before God with overflowing gratitude. Tell him every detail of your life, then God's wonderful peace that transcends human understanding, will make the answers known to you through Jesus Christ."
  Philippians 4:4-7 TPT

If something is weighing heavy on your mind.

"Lord! I'm bursting with joy over what you've done for me! My lips are full of perpetual praise. I'm boasting of you and all your works, so let all who are discouraged take heart. Join me, everyone! Let's praise the Lord together. Let's make him famous! Let's make his name glorious to all. Listen to my testimony: I cried to God in my distress, and he answered me. He freed me from all my fears!"
  Psalms 34:1-4 TPT

If you are dealing with trust.

"Pour out all your worries and stress upon him and leave them there, for he always tenderly cares for you. Be well balanced and always alert, because your enemy, the devil, roams around incessantly, like a roaring lion looking for its prey to devour. Take a decisive stand against him and resist his every attack with strong, vigorous faith. For you know that your believing brothers and sisters around the world are experiencing the same kinds of troubles you endure."
1 Peter 5:7-9 TPT

These are just a few examples of scriptures that relate to your life and some things you may be experiencing and meditate on them day and night. While doing so, know that you are in good hands and let it go. He cares for you. Therefore, cast all your care upon Him. Why carry the burdens of life when you do not have to? When you have done all, you know to do and you can do no more, relax, relate, release. Release those things that are keeping you bound, causing you to isolate yourself, the depression, anxiety, and fear; release it.

It is easy to do things in secret and, at the same time, think they will not be brought to light. One way or another, we will be affected by past and present actions. From time to time, we find ourselves insituations we are not able to crawl out of. For many reasons, some are easily persuaded, motivated by emotions, need, and acceptance. How we feel, what we want, and at times, who our friends are can put us in the line of fire. No one ever wakes up in the morning with a clear idea of exactly how their day will go, and no one ever goes to bed with a precise understanding of why. As for the type of life that Tim and Leah lead, it will continually keep them guessing from one day to the next.

At what point do we say enough is enough and turn down the volume to outside interference and only listen to God? How is it that we continue to put ourselves in awkward situations that we do not want to be in? You may be saying to yourself, *butI am human,* or *things just happen*, and I say to that, enough is enough. Sometimes that may apply, but often, we allow crazy things to happen in our lives because of the choices we make.

We can choose to say 'no', choose to walk away, and choose to control our emotions. When are we going to choose life and not death?

Does saying to yourself, *one last time or this is the last time, I promise*, ever work? Not all the time. Does it really keep us from walking into danger? Sometimes it does; however, it does not. The desire and temptation are too strong to handle on our own. We must choose light, not darkness, and in our time of transition, we need the Lord. *Release...* Look at this scripture:

"Behold, I'm standing at the door, knocking. If your heart is open to hear my voice and you open the door within, I will come in to you and feast with you, and you will feast with me."
Revelation 3:20 TPT

We must stop, quiet ourselves, and listen to the voice of God. We must choose to listen to the voice inside that tells us, *No, turn around, danger, warning!* For some, they have the flashing red light as well, and that still does not get us to listen and choose the right way.

We must choose to allow God to take us by the hand and lead us to a right path, a path where He has everything and everyone in place to help guide us through. We must choose today that God is the one we will run to and with. Do not allow the thought of, *I can do it tomorrow*, to keep you from doing what you most assuredly need to do today. There is no time to question; the time is now.

CHAPTER EIGHT

We rarely start our day with the notion that something bad is on the horizon. With no warning do we wake up knowing we will be faced with a hard choice to make. A lot of times, our day ends with several. It is up to the individual to make them good ones.

Tim never thought he would make the choice he did. Making runs for Nika during school hours, up to that point, Tim refused to do. Regardless of the doubt, Tim has always remained a runner for Nika. The ache he felt in the pit of his stomach, was never strong enough to sway him to walk away. He was raised to love the Lord with all his heart and to always seek Him for understanding. Yet he continued.

Tim sat in his car, struggling with what to do, is proof that the wrong decision was about to be made. If ever there is a doubt, God's not in it. God is not the author of confusion. Never has been and never will be. Tim knocked on the door, and Nika pulled him in.

"It took you long enough," Nika shouted throwing Tim up against the wall. "You got any weapons on you? That's an area you don't want to play in little boy."

Nika patted Tim down, and for a split second the thought of grabbing her up and becoming the next Picasso sounded grand to Tim.

Shall I make art with the color red, he thought to himself. "Nah man, I ain't got nothin' on me. Now let me go. Keep playin'."

"And what," Nika said. "What you gonna do, Little Timmy boy?"

Tim responded, "Even though you act and look like a dude, you're still a girl. Keep it up. Hurry up I got to go."

Getting right to the point, Nika asked, "You need to pick your friends up at the mall, right?"

Still a little high strung from what just took place, Tim said with much confidence. "No, I don't. I had to change my plans thanks to you."

"Okay so, you changing your plans is supposed to make me feel bad?" Nika said with no remorse. "I think not. That's where I told them to meet you in an hour."

"Why there? I'm not trying to go there to make a drop," Tim shouted.

Tim threw his hands up and walked over to the door. He thought about just leaving but he knew it was something that needed to be done.

"You were going there anyway, made perfect sense to me. Just get the job done so you can take your little girlfriend out to a movie or something."

Nika had no respect for Tim, and after what happened when he walked in, he no longer cares for her.

"Yeah, you got jokes. I would rather not be all out in the open like that. You don't understand that?"

Tim paced the floor trying to figure out how he was going to pull this off. Staying out of prison is and must always be, for Tim, the end result.

"However, you get it done is your business, just as long as it gets done. Drive around and look for a black Lincoln Navigator. I'll call him to let him know when you're coming."

Tim could not hold back any longer. Standing tall with much confidence, he took a deep breath and told Nika exactly how he felt.

"This is the last run I'm makin' for you. I'm done with this."

Nika stepped back and looked at Tim from head to toe. She walked over to her bookcase and said, "Wow, look who is getting a backbone. But you look good pumpin' your breaks. It's your pockets. If you don't wanna fill 'em, that's on you."

"I do, but not like this, not anymore. There has to be another way, and I told you this was temporary." Tim said with a sigh of relief.

"Whatever. Here's four for the last run, and two for this one," she said as if she did not believe him.

"Fine." He snatched the bag out of her hand and started walking toward the door to leave.

"Make sure you get my money andbring it back to me. Call me after the job isdone." Nika said as she grabbed him by hisshirt. "Don't make me come lookin' for you."

"I know you better back up off me, Nika. I'm not playing with you no more."

Nika pulled out her gun and pointed it toward Tim's head, "Don't start smellin' yourself, little Tim-tim. You wanna walk up out of here? Get it done. Get it done right, and get it done quick, or I WILL come find you! Now, get out of my house."

All the do's and don'ts Tim felt hit him like a freight train. It brought about a sense of urgency to run through the streets screaming. Clearly, Tim knew right from wrong; nevertheless, he refused to heed the right things. He walked out of Nika's house skeptical about how things were going to turn out, yet he refused to not go.

CHAPTER SUMMARY

Tim left Nika's house, feeling lost and with an enormous sense of regret. This is not the path he wanted to take, nor was it one he was always on. From his grandfatherto his father, running drugs for someone else to the biggest drug dealers in town were their lives, until they answered the call of The Lord. Tim had always vowed that would not be his life, as he had not always been *that guy*.

Tim had no clue what was going to go down once he reached his destination, but he continued, nevertheless. He knew in his heart he made the wrong choice to go, however turning around was not something he could do at that point. Nika made it perfectly clear she wanted her money and by any means necessary and death was not an option for him. Thoughts of how it was going to go down and what type of people he was about to meet really began to bother him. Most of Nika's clients were the same all the time. But not this time. Trying to make sure everything would go smoothly, he walked out in his mind every type of scenario and what he would need to do.

We continue to do things that we ourselves are not comfortable with, for the sake of living a lavish lifestyle, saving a friendship, or not letting someone else down. When are we going to take our lives out of the hands of man and put them in the hands of God? Think about the crazy situations that could have been avoided, the tragedies that would not have affected our lives if we just said no to the devil and yes to God. Too many times, we feel the nervous knots in our stomach. Yet, we are rolling right along, as if we have noticed nothing. When it is all said and done, when we realize that now we have to suffer the consequences, we are left wondering why and if only. When are we going to say enough is enough and choose another way, the right way? Choose now, before it is too late. Consider this scripture:

"Trust in the Lord completely, and do not rely on your own opinions. With all your heart rely on him to guide you, and he will lead you in every decision you make. Become intimate with him in whatever you do, and he will lead you wherever you go."

Proverbs 3:5-6 TPT

God would have you to choose life instead of death. You must begin to trust The Lord and believe He will never leave you; He will never abandon you. The loneliness you feel, simply put, you do not have to feel. Why, because The Lord is near. You do not have to do anything alone, but you must choose it. For some of us, if we continue to live the life we are living, we may not die physically, but we will die inside. God does not want you to succumb to your pain. There are some who have no peace and are not happy with themselves, unable to love another person. Look at this scripture:

"I hear the Lord saying, "I will stay close to you, instructing and guiding you along the pathway for your life. I will advise you along the way and lead you forth with my eyes as your guide. So don't make it difficult; don't be stubborn when I take you where you've not been before. Don't make me tug you and pull you along. Just come with me!" Lord, you are my secret hiding place, protecting me from these troubles, surrounding me with songs of gladness! Your joyous shouts of rescue release my breakthrough. Pause in his presence"
    Psalms 32:7-9 TPT

No more worrying. Worrying is not of God. No more condemning yourself, that is not okay. Condemnation is not of God. He wants us to trust Him with our whole heart and depend on Him. In The Lord, find understanding and wisdom. In Him is fullness of joy. If it is deliverance you seek, God's got you. He will help you to let go. Toxic friendships and relationships, yep He got you there, too. What college to attend, home or vehicle to purchase, rest assured, He got you. Interviewing for a position you have been praying for, no worries man, He got you. Why, because He loves you. Whatever it is you need Him to do, trust me He will do. Another scripture for you:

"So above all, constantly chase after the realm of God's kingdom and the righteousness that proceeds from him. Then all these less important things will be given to you abundantly."
Matthew 6:33 TPT

But, how will you know His voice if you do not know Him? Choose today before it is too late. Call on God to pull you out because you cannot do it in your own strength. Trust and believe, He loves you and He want to help you.

CHAPTER NINE

It was a gorgeous day, that day. The sun was shining, and the sky was clear. Tonya and Leah decided to cut the remaining two periods of school and walk to the mall. The conversation between Tonya and Leah was a good one. They were able to laugh and share stories with one another. Something they would not had been able to otherwise. Everything happens for a reason. Both were dealing with feelings of rejection, shame, and guilt that they had allowed to dominate their lives. Neither was able to really talk about it with anyone because of their fear ofbeing judged and humiliated. Neither was willing to open their hearts and allow anyone else in, until that moment. No one could get close enough to affect the negative change that was taking place inside of them. Remember God can use anyone, at any given time, in any situation to speak.

"Tonya, what's up with your girl Kim?" Leah said with a crazy look on her face.

Tonya was not sure how to answer that question. Not wanting to say the wrong thing, she stopped and took a second before responding.

"Watch yourself now. You feelin' a little free wit' ya words." Tonya said with a smirk. "Kim and I may be at odds right now, but she is my friend."

"My bad man. I ain't trippin'. I just really want to know what's up with her."

"She's deep into her church thing. What are you trying to say, Leah, for real?" Tonya began to get defensive.

"I know that's what I mean. She seems really into church, and I just don't understand why."

"So, if that's what you meant, why didn't you just say that right off the rip instead of saying what you said? What's wrong with really being into church though? Don't knock it 'til you try it Leah. Shoot, we need Jesus, too," pointed at each other, "as jacked up as we are."

"I guess. I just don't understand what it is about church that has all these people strung out on something they can't see. And I thought crack had people buggin' out. Look, I got some family who are Christians too, and they are more uptight than she is."

Leah threw her hands up as if to surrender, after getting the side eye from Tonya.

"Not saying she's uptight," Leah quickly added.

"The church that Kim goes to is cool, Leah. They got the bomb music, and the Pastor is cool, too. Real laid-back."

"Man, I just can't see going to church. There is no way. All they do is judge you and make you feel bad because you are not like them," Leah said.

"Why you say that?" Tonya said laughing.

"Why go to church, live right, do all the right things, call yourself a Christian, and still have no peace, still have problems, and still be unhappy?" Leah questioned very loudly. "That just seems silly to me, and I can't see putting myself through all those changes for nothing."

Leah knows absolutely nothing about the grace and mercy of God. It is funny how there are those who do not know the inner workings of a Christian's life, yet they think they know so much.

"Leah, where is this coming from? You can't judge all of Christianity by just the people you know. Your family is crazy. I mean *really toe-up*. How do you know what goes on in a Christian's life?"

"I got family." Leah said as she rolled her eyes.

"Clearly," Tonya said. "See, that's what I'm saying. Your family ain't wrapped too tight anyway, man." Tonya laughed so hard that Leah began to feel some type of way. "We all have people in our family that either play church, run to the church, or can't run away fast enough from the church."

What are you going to do about your life? What type of family member are you? We should never base our lives and perception about Christianity on anyone but The Lord.

"Anyway, I'm fine. Things are okay with me." Leah said.

"Yeah, for the moment. There's a scripture in the Bible that says that it rains on the just and on the unjust. Now, I believe that means that you're going to go through stuff whether you're a Christian or not. The difference is that you'll either go through it with God or without Him." Tonya said.

"But, Tonya, man, I would have to stop smokin' and partyin', and that just can't happen."

They laughed so hard at what Leah said that everyone outside turned around and stared at them. Almost to their destination, Tonya and Leah decided to sit outside to finish talking before going in to eat. The conversation took a turn that neither one predicted.

Tonya looked around and noticed what a nice day it was. For a brief moment she thought about how sad her home life really was.

In a depressing tone, Tonya said, "It is such a nice day. I wish it was as beautiful at home as it is out here right now."

Not sure she heard Tonya correctly, Leah stopped and jumped in front of herand asked, "What?"

"Nothing. You don't think you would ever go to church, not even once?" Tonya said trying to change the subject.

Leah started cracking up and asked, "You ever seen that movie The Exorcist?"

"Yeah, I have." Tonya looked at her strangely and asked, "Why?"

"Yeah, well, that would be me. Not good for anyone." Leah shook her head. "Not good. Come on, let's sit down right here. Shoot, I smoke. I need to rest for a minute."

"Leah let's sit here in the shade. I'm not trying to get a tan today." As they sat on the ground, Tonya said to Leah, "To me, church is like a hospital where sick or terminally ill people go."

Leah wasn't sure where Tonya was going. "How so? I think I know what you're trying to say, but you explain it to me," she said.

"Think about it, sick people, hospital, sinners, and church. You follow me? I think sin is like a sickness or disease and trials are like an infection, to Christians, and God's house is a place to go to be healed or delivered from that sickness or sin. What I'm trying to say Leah, is that you need Jesus," Tonya explained patting on Leah's shoulder.

Leah chuckled and looked at Tonya with a serious look on her face and replied, "Girl, you do too," patting Tonya on her knee.

The girls looked at each other and at the same time and busted out laughing.

"You do the same things I do," Leah said. "I get it though, Tonya. I know what you mean."

"I sure do. I'm jacked up too, shoot. It's hard to make it in this world without divine help. This world is a mess, and we're both a mess, too. Our issues are deep, and we can't maintain without God's help, Leah. I don't know about you, but I'm going through hell right now, and I need help."

Leah understands, but at the same time, she is looking at Tonya crazy because she can't quite understand why.

What is making Tonya come from such a place? This is the same girl that smoked weed with Leah, the same girl that she drank with. She can't be talking about God, right? What He can do and where to go to find a healing. Or can she?

"I get it, girl," Leah said, while waving her hand vigorously. "This is a little too deep for me. I'm still high, girl."

Tonya and Leah have been talking for so long, they forgot about Tim. After a while, Tonya began to get suspicious and asked questions.

"So, what were you and Tim supposed to do today?" Tonya asked.

Leah answered, "Nothing you need to worry about. I just can't do it without him.

Tonya was curious and tried her best to pull information out of Leah. But Leah would not dare tell.

"It seems very important to you."

"I'm just gonna wait until he comes with me. It is important, but it can wait. But anyway, I just need a heads-up when you go that deep, girl. You know what I'm saying? What I wanna talk about is this church. Is it fun? 'Cause you know, I gotta have fun. I might have to check it out."

"You should check it out. Hold up though, that was way too quick. You're real indecisive sometimes, huh, Leah? Not that I'm not happy that you want to. But dang!"

"Shut up girl," Leah said. "Anyway, I enjoy kickin' it and hangin' out with my friends. Don't get me wrong. It would be hard for me to quit doin' certain things I do, but the more you said and the more I think about it, the more I know I need more."

We now know, not wanting to be transparent is a quality Tonya and Leah share. It's for certain. What will transpire next, they will never see coming.

"I know what you mean," Tonya said. "It's still hard for me to be able to fully let go of my will and give it to someone else. That is not an easy thing to do for anyone. But keep in mind that it will not happen overnight. I have done so much dirt, and you have done so much dirt and know that dirt will not clear overnight. Not saying that God can't fix it in a blink of an eye, but let's be realistic.

We have been living foul for a long time. It's possible for God to get exhausted from clearing our dirt away," Tonya said as she laughed. "I'm just playing. The great thing is He allows us the choice, and that's what I love about God. He doesn't force you to do anything."

"But Tonya, you know I have a lot of friends and we have fun, but all we do is smoke and drink. Girl, I never thought I would get tired of smoking weed." Leah said. "That is just crazy to me. Who does that? I've been smoking for so long. I don't know anything else, really."

Leah laughed, but nothing changed the fact that this was a serious situation and the more they talked the more they realized that living without God is a serious offense and something they should no longer do. It goes without saying, these are not feelings that Leah could see having at any given moment, and Tonya never thought she would ever have a conversation of this magnitude with Leah.

"Very true, Leah, and at the end of the day, what do you have?" Tonya asked.

"A hangover and a bad headache. That's what you have," Leah chuckled. "I feel you, Tonya, man. All I know is I can't keep livin' like this. Something's gotta give. I know a change will not happen quickly,but you know what, that would be okay with me. I'm so messed up it could be a long transformation."

Tonya giggled and said, "You are so crazy girl. At least, you will know it would happen at some point. Life would be so much better though."

"Yeah, less cloudy and no hangover headaches," Leah said.

The girls laughed so hard Tonya fell off the curb. You know, it was one of those laughs that have you saying, *man, I needed that laugh*. Yep, one of those.

"And, Leah, there would be nothing to hide from people. Once I give it to God, I'm good. As long as I have His forgiveness, I could care less about what other people say or think about me."

Both girls let out a sigh of relief. To be able to let go of some of the pain was what they needed. They got up and began walking again. Quietly, they continued down the street. The closer they got, the deeper the silence grew. All of a sudden, Leah stopped, stood with her hands on her hips for a moment, and a tear ran down her face. Tonya turned to look at Leah, gave her a hug, and said nothing. Leah took a long deep breath and wiped her face.

"You know, if there were people to help me, I think I could do it," Leah said softly. "Because you know, I'm so jacked up, I'ma need the priest, the pope, the bishop, and elders and the deacons to cast this demon out."

"Don't you mean, these demons? Oh wait, I believe they are called legions," Tonya laughed so hard she ran into a trash can.

Leah helped to keep Tonya from falling and said, "That's what you get. God don't like ugly."

"How about we help each other," Tonya said, "with God's help, of course? We can hold each other accountable. We both need to change."

"You got that right," Leah said. "Plus, I see how happy Kim is, and I want that happiness for myself. But I'm just not sure I want to jump through hoops to get there."

"If you want it bad enough, you'll do what you gotta do to get it." Tonya expressed.

"One day at a time, sweet Jesus," Leah sang in a loud voice.

Tonya chuckled and said, "Why you have to sing it like a country singer though, Leah? Girl, I can't breathe. You are too much. I'm done laughing at you. You wanna go inside to eat now? I'm hungry."

"Yeah, let's go. We can get our food and come back out here and eat. Is that cool?" Leah asked.

"That's cool. Not too happy about that decision, but it's warm out. I hate eating outside."

Tonya, do I wanna know?"

"I don't do well with bugs." Tonya said as if she was really grossed out.

"Girl, who does?" Leah said laughingly.

"Crazy people," Tonya said.

"Come on weirdo, let's go."

CHAPTER SUMMARY

The more Tonya and Leah talked about their home lives, the more helpless they both felt. Neither knew what to say and confirmed that without a doubt their lives had to change. Soon they would be graduating and begin a new chapter or phase of their lives. They also knew that even though they did not have parents at home that truly loved them the way they thought parents should, they had a Heavenly Father who would love them unconditionally, and with His help they could be better people.

Sniff after every uncontrollable sniff, the girls were able to pull themselves together. They chose to continue talking because they knew it was something they needed, if to only release. People are put in place, with like experiences when it is needed. They promised themselves not to let their problems rule their lives any longer.

Even in our disobedience and our unfaithfulness, He is still faithful and true to His Word.

Even when we think He is not there and working on your behalf, He is. God used Tonya, through her experience with Him to encourage Leah.

You must have a willing heart and run after all God has for you. Once you are willing to say, *enough is enough*, I do not want to go through this alone," open your heart, seek God, and everything He has for you will be yours. Everything that He has can belong to you as well.

[5] "You can be sure that I have heard the groans of the people of Israel, who are now slaves to the Egyptians. And I am well aware of my covenant with them.[6] "Therefore, say to the people of Israel: 'I am the LORD. I will free you from your oppression and will rescue you from your slavery in Egypt. I will redeem you with a powerful arm and great acts of judgment. [7] I will claim you as my own people, and I will be your God. Then you will know that I am the LORD your God who has freed you from your oppression in Egypt. [8] I will bring you into the land I swore to give to Abraham, Isaac, and Jacob. I will give it to you as your very own possession. I am the LORD!"

Exodus 6:5-8 NLT

"Remember, you are not, will not, and never will be alone. Open your heart and know that I will be with you always," says God. You need to have peace in your life. Never forget that you will have trials and you will go through stuff but take heart. It's okay because the Lord has overcome the world.

The Lord has already suffered, bled, and died for you. Now, it is up to you. You have to have a willing heart that is open to receive. You have to forgive so you can be forgiven. Just think about it. You owe yourself that much to at least think about it. You certainly have nothing to lose by thinking about what God has done. In Tonya and Leah's conversation on their walk to the mall, not only were their issues and struggles being revealed to one another, but healing was beginning to take place.

CHAPTER TEN

In a matter of minutes, the sky was full of clouds and there was an eerie feeling in the air. The sun disappeared and the sound of happy chirping birds were no more. Some stood staring at the sky clinching their bags, jackets, and children and some quickly walked to their cars. Tonya and Leah did not mind the way things looked outside. They sat down at the picnic table picking up where they left off in their conversation.

Purging is not just for the cleansing of your physical body. I have found it also helps the mind and spirit. Guilt, the feeling of rejection, depression, and shame, reminds me of bondage. It is like being in prison, and one of the things that can free you is simply talking about it and letting go. However, that is not all it entails to be free. Not only do you have to loosen your grip of the issues, but you must also release them into the right hands—the only one who can truly make them dissipate. And it does not stop there. Once you loosen and then release, God can fill the empty places with His grace, mercy, favor, and agape love which are of and from God, whose very nature is love.

With a lot of emotion, Leah said, "Tonya, man, my mom and dad are crazy. They smoke all the time, and they drink. I'm amazed they can even hold down jobs. I either stay in my room or I'll just leave the house because I don't want to deal with it, and I don't like seeing them that way."

"You know, I was wondering why you were never at home whenever I stopped by. That's crazy. I don't know what I'd do if I had to deal with parents who did those things. I can't see my parent's doing drugs."

"Girl, I can't wait until graduation, 'cause I'm out," Leah said. "They are the reason I started smoking in the first place. They could care less that it affects me. To be completely honest, they probably don't even notice. They pay no attention to me whatsoever."

"How you figure that?" Tonya asked. "I'm sure if they knew you were partying like you do, they would not be too happy."

Leah's voice began to quiver. Everything that Leah and Tonya had been discussing began to make Leah very emotional. Her body language and demeanor slowly began to change.

"Maybe not. Think about it. They do it all the time. I grew up watching them," Leah explained. "It's not like they tried to hide it and it's not like it's weed. They do the hard stuff. They don't care. They would do it right in front of me."

"Dang girl. I thought I had it bad. I don't even know what to say," Tonya said.

"What can anyone say really? It's like I was hooked as a child," Leah whispered. "Now . . . well, you know. They didn't hurt me by hitting me, but they did hurt me though. Getting me hooked on this. It's crazy, man. Now, I can't kick the habit. I feel like a weed junky, and trust, it will not go any further than that. Ain't no gateway goin' on here."

Tonya stood up and walked to the end of the sidewalk and began to tell Leah in a somber voice, her parents were separated. Soon Leah would come to understand just how much they had in common. Tonya does have both parents at home, but it is not the same, it is almost roommate in nature. Her father sleeps in another room, and he had people over all hours of the day and night. Her mother was hardly ever home.

Tonya dealt with her parents constantly fighting, and her grades were slipping. She had no desire to be in school anymore, and until today, she has had no one to talk to. Yes, she had Kim as a friend, but there is a fear of what Kim will say or think about her. Tonya is afraid of being judged by Kim or anyone else.

"Leah, I hate my life," Tonya shrieked and scared the crap out of Leah. "*And* the reality of it is there's nothing I can do about it. My dad constantly tells me everything is my fault. Which I don't understand, I ain't married to her. I feel so helpless when I am home. I have no control over anything. What am I going to do?"

"Girl, I have no idea. I'm in the same boat you're in, remember?" Leah said. "We both jacked up."

"And people wonder why we run to the streets. Because we got it bad at home, no love, no respect, but we can sho nuff find it in the streets. We are constantly being told we won't amount to anything, be anything, and have anything, by our parents. How can anyone deal with that?" Tonya said.

Tonya was surprised to see Leah crying because she comes off as being hard and unmoved by anything. With everything in her, Tonya tried to be strong for Leah. She began to tremble. The pain of her issues engulfed Leah's very being like a tsunami. She quickly broke down.

"For me, the bad thing about it is that my father doesn't act like a father," Tonya said. "He has no clue whether I come or go, and he won't let my mother love me the way she should."

"*Please*, what is that? A mother's love, hmm. I have not had that in so long," Leah said in a sarcastic tone. "I don't know what it is anymore, a mother's love, a father's love, whatever to that."

Continuing where she left off, Tonya said, "Well, it would be a lot easier to deal with. I wouldn't keep asking myself what I did wrong. The worse thing is—"

"There's a worse thing?" Leah interrupted. "It doesn't get any worse than that, I think."

Tonya said after taking another deep breath, "The worse thing is that I hate my life, Leah, and I don't like that. I refuse to end up like my parents, with nothing.

What I mean by nothing is being empty inside, no love, no compassion for another person, namely me!"

"I hate my home life, too and the things I do, but I told you I don't know anything else. That's why it is so hard for me to change. You're not the only one. That's all I have to say," Leah told Tonya.

"Only one what, Leah?" Tonya asked for clarification.

Leah began to laugh hysterically and said, "The only one with Jerry Springer drama in their life."

Tonya and Leah were able to laugh, and in the midst of it all, they began to feel a little bit better.

"Tonya, I kinda had a feeling something was going on because you've changed. You were goin' to church all the time. You seemed really into it, happy and free. Before you smiled all the time, you looked happy, must have been a front."

"I'm going to change the subject for a second. Leah, why do you hang out with Tim?"

"Tonya—He takes care of me. You know how my parents are. Tim and I are like brother and sister. He looks out for me. Tim got caught up in some mess last year, and he has to work it off. That is one of the reasons why he is doin' what he's doin' now.

That's why I didn't complain too much when he said he had to go make a run. I just hope he is okay. It's never taken this long before, and I haven't heard from him."

"I would hate for something to happen to him," Tonya said. "Could you imagine turning on the news and hearing one of your friends had been hurt or killed? So much crazy stuff goes on in these streets. You just never know. God please . . ."

Leah looked at Tonya with an inquisitive look on her face and asked, "Can God really hear you when you talk to him?"

"Yeah, I know He can," Tonya replied.

Tonya found it very refreshing that Leah was asking questions.

"Hmm, but how do you really know that though?" Leah said suspiciously.

"I know because He said so. There is a scripture in the, um— I don't know—I don't know what it says word for word either, but it talks about Jesus saying to have faith in God and all you have to do is believe and do not doubt in your heart. You can pray for anything, and if you believe, you will have it. So, I believe He can hear whatever you say, ask, or think."

"Well, then"—Leah chuckled—"He knows I need help."

"He's all knowing, Leah, and He sees all things. We all need help. Even those who are saved need help to stay saved. Nothing is easy and nothing is free."

"I feel ya girl. Come on, Tonya. I wanna go inside and call Tim. Gotta make sure my boy is okay."

Leah and Tonya started walking toward the mall. Before they could get to the door, Tonya could hear arguing coming from the back of the parking lot. She stopped and turned her ear toward that direction

---

"You think you slick? That ain't all of it," the voice shouted.

Leah continued walking and talking, not realizing Tonya was not beside her. Confused, she turned to see where she went.

"Girl don't be havin' me talkin' to myself. What are you doin'?"

Tonya wanted to make sure she was not going crazy. Hoping she wasn't, she asked Leah if she heard voices coming from the middle of the parking lot.

"No, I didn't hear anything. You all right? I'm startin' to worry about you."

Leah looked at Tonya strangely and continued walking toward the mall.

"I don't know what you're talkin' about, but you need to bring it down a few notches," the voice said again.

"I know you heard it that time, Leah? It sounded like people arguing. Let's go. I don't need any more drama in my life. Let's go inside the mall," Tonya said softly.

"Girl, why are you whispering? Come on Tonya, let's go see. I loves me a good fight, especially the fights we don't have to pay to see," Leah jerked Tonya's arm, hoping that would get her to go.

Tonya responded yelling, "No! I'm not going anywhere. My life may be jacked up right now, but dang, Leah, you don't even know who it is. Use your head. I thought you wanted to go call Tim anyway." Tonya said.

Tonya began to make her way toward the mall, hoping Leah would follow. Leah pulled on Tonya's arm again, nearly dragging her in the direction of the voices.

"Come on Tonya. I'm not going by myself, and there's no one else out here to go with me. So that leaves you."

Leah gave Tonya's arm one more good yank and just about pulled it out the socket.

"Leah, I don't want to go down there," Tonya said as loud as she could, whispering no longer expressed her feelings in that moment. "Why do you want to go anyway? You don't know who it is, and it may not be safe! Stop acting crazy. Bring your butt on here. See that's how people get shot, being in the wrong place at the wrong time, when you should be minding your own business, going inside this mall to call Tim."

"Come on chicken, stop all that squawkin' and let's go," Leah laughed at Tonya so hard.

She will soon realize why Tonya's choice was the wisest one.

"Whatever, I'm going, you can stay here! But stay right here though, Tonya, soI can see you, better yet, so you can see me."

"Right, so I can see you get your head blown off 'cause you're being stupid and nosey. Yeah, that makes perfect sense," Tonya said sarcastically. "Leah, do you hear yourself," pointing at her ears, "speak sometimes? You make absolutely no sense to me."

Leah left Tonya standing on the sidewalk to get a little closer to the voices. As she got closer, she realized it was Tim, and he was with someone she had never seen before. Leah yelled down to Tonya, letting her know it was Tim. Tonya did not want to get caught in the middle of someone else's argument. However, Leah was very adamant that it was Tim, and once Tonya heard the urgency in Leah's voice, she ran down to where she was. Not at all how the girls wanted to spend their afternoon.

Leah said to Tonya, "It's Tim, and we need to see what's up."

"It doesn't feel right, Leah," Tonya expressed. "Something's about to go down, and you shouldn't be there when it happens."

"That's my boy Tonya. You can stand here if you want. I'm going!"

Tonya did not feel comfortable with getting in the middle of Tim's battle, nor did she want Leah to go alone. Tonya sensed a deep heaviness all around her. Something was stirring in the atmosphere, and Tonya could feel it. Something so thick you could cut it with a knife.

Very still, Tonya stood behind Leah, and with a confused look on her face, Tonya saw more than she wanted to see.

More than two people, Tonya thought to herself. *This can't be.*

Tonya tried to reach for Leah's arm, but unable to move, she stood motionless. Leah stepped closer to Tim and asked what was going on and what was with all the arguing. Tonya noticed one guy standing in front of Tim and shook her head rapidly to snap out of it.

With a perplexed look on her face she asked, "Don't we know you? Don't you go to our school?" Then she turned around and asked Leah, "Don't we—"

Very surprised, Tim interrupted Tonya, shouting, "Where did you two come from? Leah, you two shouldn't be out here."

"First of all, I should be askin' the questions. Secondly, we have been here for a while, chillin.' Third, you play us, and you're asking us what we're doin' out here," Leah yelled back at Tim. "But whatever to that, what is going on here? Who is this?"

Tim knew if he did not do something drastic, Leah would not get the point and leave. He pushed her shoulder and yelled to take Tonya and go inside the mall. The dealer could care less about the girls being there.

He jumped in between Leah and Tim to make his point that he was short a bag. The dealer kept his back toward Tonya because he did not want her to realize she did indeed know him.

"Excuse me!" the dealer yelled. "I hate to break up your little reunion here. Don't let me have to say this again. You short me a bag, and you will do somethin' about this now." Tim pointed in the dealer's face and started to say something completely disrespectful. He could only think about getting the girls away from his argument before something crazy happened.

"I said wait a minute," Tim shouted. "Let me get my friends out of here first."

"Leah, come on. I want to go, *please*!" Tonya shouted frantically, pulling on Leah's arm, and Leah yanked it away.

Emotions were running high, and no one was going to back down. Leah was going to stand by her friend at all costs; no matter what the cost. That right there will preach. If we would only do the same for God.

Insisting on staying, Leah said, "Short a bag! What is he talking about Tim? Is this what you had to do today, why you changed plans with Tonya and me? Ain't this some crap to come out here and have to deal with one of Willy Wonka's Oompa Loompas?"

"Excuse me," the dealer said in disgust.

Leah turned around and looked at him and said, "I'm just sayin'. Look at you. You got on like three different colors though, little man."

"Leah, quit playin'," Tim said spinning her around to face him. "I don't have to explain anything to you," Tim said. "Don't let me have to tell you again! This is not the time or the place for you two to be out here. Take your butts"—he points—"inside the mall now, and I'm as serious as I have ever been!"

"Did you not hear me?" A very irritated dealer pushed Tim to get his attention. "Do I need to talk a little louder, Tim tim? You short me a bag, and we *will* deal with this *right* now, not later! No one is leaving until I have what I came here for and it's just as simple as that. If I have to draw blood, then so be it!"

This so-called drug dealer is not at all who Tim thinks he is and is indeed who Tonya thinks he could be. He is a student at the same high school they all attend.

"I *wish* you would my man. You most assuredly *do not* know me dog, and you don't want to go down that rabbit hole. I will get my Lady and my best friend out of here."

Leah looked at Tonya and mouthed, *lady*. Then looked at Tim with her mouth wide open. All the while Tonya stood quietly with her head tilted, squinting, trying to understand what she was seeing, completely clueless about what was just said.

"You sure you wanna make that move bro?" Tim said, putting his hand around his back.

Tim was ready to do whatever necessary to protect himself and the girls. He stepped closer to the dealer. Tim was infuriated with Leah and Tonya.

"If you don't like it, take your little bit of money and go the heck on!"

Tim turned toward Leah, grabbed her, and pleaded with her to let him handle his business and to leave before things between him and the dealer got any worse. He remembered the funny feeling he had in the car on the way to the mall. He knew it was not going to end well.

A motionless Tonya stood in one spot while Tim and the dealer were going back and forth. Leah's emotions were all over the place.

"I need you to take Tonya inside the mall now, please!" Tim stressed.

"I don't know why you keep sayin' that man. It's evident I'm not going anywhere," Leah said disregarding what Tim wanted.

"Leah, I need you to get my girl out of here."

Your girl, Tonya said to herself. Putting her hand on Leah's shoulder to help persuade Leah to leave. "Let him handle his business," her voice shook in fear.

Tim refused to budge, and the dealer wanted to keep things moving, the tension escalated. Clouds rolled in layer by amazing layer, and the sky darkened by the minute.

Out of the corner of her eye, Tonya saw an image wearing a very dark robe, no hands, and no face, but Tonya knew it noticed her. She could feel the hopelessness and death it expelled.

"Nothing about this moment screams positivity," Tonya cried to Leah. "I can hear it, but I can't make out what it's saying though."

"What are you talking about, Tonya?" Leah asked.

"Never mind," Tonya held Leah's hand for dear life.

Whisper after demonic whisper, it began to lurk between Tim and the drug dealer, rubbing its hands together, pointing, and laughing.

Lord what am I seein'? Is this for real? This doesn't happen to me, Tonya thought to herself. *Why did You pick me, Lord? This is crazy. Like, I don't know how to take this. I know we need to go inside. I know something is about to happen. I know that much. This some craziness right here, I don't know what to do, oh my God, I don't know what to do. I gotta get the heck away from here, but I can't move. Oh my God my feet won't move from this here spot.*

"I'm not goin' anywhere. You go ahead finish what you're doin'," Leah screamed. "You waistin' time askin' me to roll out. I'm not, so keep it movin'." Turning to Tonya, Leah said in a serious tone, "Tonya . . . Tonya, can you hear me? She done went into shock. Lawd help us all."

What was only a few seconds felt like hours to Tonya. It was as though time stopped for a moment. On the right of them, stood an image in an all-white, neatly pressed hooded robe. She noticed the beautiful golden belt around its waist. Tonya knew without a doubt the black image represented evil and hell and the white image represented good and heaven. The white image stood with its head down in one place, motionless most of the time. The black image walked around as though it was orchestrating the whole incident.

My feet won't move, and I can't get Leah to leave if my own feet won't move from the spot, they're in, Tonya said to herself. *I feel like it's about to happen. It's so heavy on me, like it's sitting on my shoulders, Lord. My heart is beating so fast, I can't breathe. Why do they keep arguing? Why can't the dealer feel that big thing all up on him? It's like right there all up on him. He can't feel that thing breathin' down his neck. Scream stupid. This is crazy. What is it doing to them? It better not come over here, waving nothing around me. I know that much.*

Tonya heard nothing Leah was saying to her. In a trance, frozen, she wondered why the white image did nothing. It allowed the black image to wreak havoc all around them.

"Look, you need to call Nika about this. I'm just the runner. She short you, not me," Tim shouted to the dealer.

"This has something to do with Nika?" Leah said to Tim in disbelief. "I should have known. She played you Tim. She set you up. I told you she was shady, but no, you just had to keep doin' business with her."

"Nah, we're gonna take care of this right now," the dealer dropped the bag of drugs and reached his hand around his back. Pointing at Tim, he said, "Get it together, my man, right now!"

"He said take it up with Nika!" Leah screamed.

"What is your name? Leah?" The dealer asked.

"Yeah, why?" Leah answered.

The dealer walked up to Leah and the black image was stuck to him like glue. "Well then, Miss Leah, I don't think I was talking to you!" He said giving her a look that could kill.

Leah said, not backing down, "But I'm pretty sure I was talkin' to you. You don't scare me. Don't act like you're out here intimidating somebody, 'cause you're not." She stared him down, unwavering, and confident.

"Leah, shut your mouth! Why are you still here, anyway? I can't do this with you out here." Tim yelled to her yet again.

"Well, you might as well 'cause I'm not going anywhere! Nope, I'm not leavin' you out here with this non-dressin', last-year's-Jordans-wearin', wannabe drug dealer. No! Get it out your crazy freakin' mind."

The white image lifted its head, Tonya moved her head at the same time, and the black image stood completely still. Tonya noticed the glow coming from inside the hood of the white image.

"Come on, Leah," Tonya never took her eyes away from the direction of the images. "I really think we need to go. For real, something is coming," Tonya said softly.

Tonya felt a warm tingling sensation all through her body. There was an enormous amount of commotion going on in the natural, and a battle between good and evil was taking place in the spiritual. The images were on opposite sides of each other. Good on the right and evil on the left. Tonya knew at that very moment that a battle was about to begin.

"Little girl, you need to listen to your friend and leave before you get hurt out here," the dealer said to Leah.

Leah's response was not of a female who would back down from a challenge. "I got your little girl, and I said I'm not going anywhere!"

"I don't think you guys know who you're dealin' with, little Tim-tim," the dealer said in a snarling tone.

The black image moved to the back of the dealer, and the dealer reached his hand behind his back, yet again.

The black image raised its left hand, and the dealer pulled out his gun.

"Oh, for real, that's what we doin' now!" Leah said.

"Oh God," Tonya shouted.

The black image raised its other hand and pointed, and the dealer pointed the gun at Tim at the same time.

"Tonya, get your girl and leave right now! I am not gonna tell you again!"

The black image stood motionless in one spot, with its arms pointed in the direction of Tim and the girls. The white image slowly moved in front of Tonya and Leah. Now remember, the only one who can see the images was Tonya.

Tim knew at that moment things were about to go all bad for them. The dealer was not playing anymore; he wanted what he wanted, and either he was going to get it, or someone was going to die. Tim turned to look at Tonya and noticed the strange look on her face. He grabbed her arms, shook her, and got no reaction. He put one arm around her waist, pulled her to him, looked her in the eyes, and whispered.

"Tonya, what is wrong with you? What are you lookin' at?" He asked again, "Tonya, what is wrong? Snap out of it, babe please!"

The white image stretched out its arm to the right, and Tonya turned her head in that direction. Tim continued talking to Tonya and with the other arm reached around his back and pulled out his gun. With no response from Tonya, he quickly turned and shielded her.

"I don't think you want it to go down like this, little Tim-tim," the dealer said. "Put the gun down before you or, better yet, your little girl friends get killed out here."

"Think about this, bro. I hope you know what you're about to do. I ain't puttin' nothin' down, but I think you should if you want to live! Now, I told you I had nothing to do with this. If you have a problem, take it up with Nika. She shorted you, not me!"

The white image looked up and pointed to the sky and Tonya fell to the ground, simultaneously the black image stretched both his arms as wide as could be, smacked them both together, and three gunshots rang through the air. The white image disappeared and left behind nothing but total darkness. As Tim, Leah, and Tonya lay on the ground, the black image continued walking in a circle around them, laughing as if its plan worked.

Choices. The choices that people make in their everyday lives. What do you choose?—The black image said walking around them as they lay on the ground.— *Have you ever been in a situation like this? Maybe you have. No one really knows about Tim's home life. What would lead him to a life of crime? He was a youth minister and Christian artist, just a year ago. What about this wanna be drug dealer?*—It points as he lay on the ground. *—His father a pastor, a PK they say, I love those the most. I love that he chose to sell drugs and willing to help me take lives. I made sure their parents were too preoccupied to even notice the things they do. Making sure no one is the wiser about their precious little children. You would think they would notice their children are bruised and hurting, but they do not, I made sure of that, too. When they are rejected at home, do not worry, parents, I am here to welcome them with open arms. I will take care of them. Just you wait and see.*

Young or old, you all must make choices every day to do the right things and say the right things; you and I both know that. It is hard to be a good Christian, or it is no fun to be a Christian, I have heard some say.

All I can say when I hear that is, really, well I am here to help and make it more difficult for you. These are some of your reasons for not wanting to follow Jesus. I love that people choose to serve me, to run with me— the black image snarled—I am good at what I do, the black image said as it laughed and took its bow.

The devil knows your weaknesses and will do whatever necessary to get you off track, surround you with things that are not good for you, and alienate you from all things good. Are you going to continue the path you are on or are you going to respond to The Lord?

CHAPTER SUMMARY

I would like for you to try something with me. Close your eyes and envision your life, examine it and the choices you have made. Can you honestly say that everything you have done lines up with what God says, His will, and His plan? All right, now watch, I am going somewhere with this. The black image may have succeeded, as the evidence was lying on the ground. There are people who sell drugs, prostitute themselves, maybe even commit other crimes according to the laws of the land. There are others who, steal, kill, commit adultery, the list goes on and on—we all know that. You may not identify with this list, nevertheless we all have sinned at some point in our lives, according to the scripture.

"If we boast that we have no sin, we're only fooling ourselves and are strangers to the truth."
1 John 1:8 TPT

"for we all have sinned and are in need of the glory of God. Yet through his powerful declaration of acquittal, God freely gives away his righteousness. His gift of love and favor now cascades over us, all because Jesus, the Anointed One, has liberated us from the guilt, punishment, and power of sin!"

Romans 3:23-24 TPT

Tonya, Tim, and the dealer have all had relationships with The Lord, at one point or another. However, something happened that changed all of that. Their own personal story, their guilt, shame, and sin were the catalyst along the way that changed their hearts and minds. This too may be someone else's truth. We must understand that sin opens the door for so much more than a trip to a hospital, prison or maybe even the grave. Sin opens the door for more sin, sickness, pain, and finally, eternal death. Trust me, this cycle will never change unless we are willing to change, and unless we are willing to change, living life become so much harder to live.

What we all must do is realize that the things we are doing are not of God, pray and ask God to forgive us, repent and sin no more. I must tell myself all the time that a change will not happen overnight, although I wish it would. Know that once you say yes, you must continue to say yes.

Daily you will be tempted, daily you will be reminded of your failings, daily you may need to be lifted up, and daily you must say yes and wait. Please know, all sins are equal in that sin no matter what it is, divides us from God. All sin, whether it is sin in your heart, whether you sin with your mouth or with your physical body.

There are so many choices that people make that are not of God. How will your life end? Choices! The good thing is that all those things can be forgiven. You can be forgiven; you just must choose whose side you want to be on.

If you no longer want to be among those who sin. If you no longer want to be among those who do not truly have a relationship with God. If you want to always be in God's Will. If you want to receive the Lord into your heart and know Him for yourself, turn away from sin and sin no more; say this prayer with me.

Dear father, I believe that Jesus Christ is Your only begotten Son, and that He came down to earth in the flesh and died on the cross to take away all of my sins. I believe that Jesus Christ rose from the dead that I would have eternal life. Lord Jesus, I confess to you all of the wrong and sinful things I have ever done in my life. I ask that you please forgive me and wash them all away by the blood you shed for me on the cross. I am ready to accept You into my life and into my heart. I want to have a personal relationship with you Lord Jesus and You to live with me for all eternity. Father, I believe that I am truly saved and born again, and I thank You for accepting me.

If you believe it from your heart, you have become saved and born again. Now go and sin no more. Welcome into the Body of Christ!

CHAPTER ELEVEN

Kim left her car at school and walked home to think. Halfway to her destination, she thought about her mother Jody and how she would react if she cut school. It was not hard for her to figure out Tonya left, as she never showed up for Study Hall. Deciding to take the long way home, Kim wanted to walk through the park. She sat down at a picnic table and pulled out her notebook.

Mom would not be happy with me if I cut school, she thought to herself. *I would come up missin' for sure. Oh my gosh, she knows everything. There is absolutely no way she would not figure out something's up, and she knows Tonya's mother—she* thought grabbing her chest—*and mom is crazy, she will call her mom, I know it. Heck yeah, she would. I need to get it together before I get home because that just cannot happen. She is a Christian, but a Christian woman that don't play*, Kim thought to herself.

Opening the pages to where she left off the day before, Kim continued to write. *Like, there's no break in thought or feelings, so easy I pick up where I left off. Out of control, my mind spins like a merry-go-round. These feelings aren't emotions I want to have, dizzy from the chaos all around me. No longer am I in the middle of the tornado where it is calm, and I am safe from the chaos outside.*

Now, I am dizzy from the chaos that is on the inside of me. The constant turning and being jostled about, issue after uncontrollable issue, never different, always the same, constant. A constant reminder,

but the outcome never seems to change. Round and round and round I go, my next stop, hey what do ya know! I'll fix you up nice and pretty, since you want to coexist.

"Mom can smell trouble a mile away. Let me get home before she starts trippin' about me walking in later than usual. 'You might be a senior in high school, but don't get it twisted up in through here,' she always says. Mom cracks me up," Kim said to herself.

Kim made it home and with a plan on how to sneak in. She put one hand on the top of the front door and the other on the doorknob to minimize the noise, so she thought. Kim slid in the house, turned, and shut the door. She tried to tiptoe upstairs to her room, *nope, that didn't work*, she thought to herself.

"Kim, is that you? I know she did not... Kim!" Jody yelled from the living room.

"Dang it. That usually works. See that dang nose. I promise she's a bloodhound. Either that nose or those supersonic ears. I can't even sneak in the house."

Kim put her book bag on the floor, by the bottom of the stairs, knocked out the imaginary person standing in front of her, and started toward the living room.

"Chloe, go see if that was Kim that came in," Jody said. "How is she going to come in here all late and not say anything?"

Chloe, like any other little sister, loved to get Kim into trouble. Their relationship was like any other sibling relationship. They argue and pick fights with each other constantly, but no one else could, that's for sure. Chloe will always take advantage of any opportunity to mess with Kim.

"You can't hear," Chloe said to Kim, "Mommy wants you. You better come on before you get into trouble. I'm gonna tell her you tried to sneak in the house, too."

"Whatever, Chloe! Just go tell Mom I'm coming," Kim said as she pushed Chloe out of the way. "I'm going to put my stuff in my room first. Stop acting like a little brat."

Kim walked into her room and closed the door. Leaning back on the door, Kim tossed her bag on the bed and slid to the floor. Minutes went by, and Chloe was knocking to get Kim to come downstairs.

"Mommy called you like two times," Chloe said. "You better come on. What's wrong with you? You better get it together before you get down there. I know that's right."

"I know, Chloe," Kim said pushing Chloe out her room.

Kim walked down the hall trying to shake off all the worry and tension she was feeling. She walked into the living room and sat down on the edge of the couch.

"Hey, Mom. I just got here."

Looking at Kim strangely, Jody replied, "Hello there. I thought I heard you come in."

Chloe sat down on the floor by Jody and started reading a book. Looking up at Kim, she asked, "What about me?"

"What about you?" Kim responded.

"You didn't say hi to me," Chloe said.

Kim rolled her eyes at Chloe and whispered, "I don't like you."

"Kim, I heard that. I know you didn't think you were whispering. Don't talk to your sister that way," Jody said in her firm voice.

"But she just stuck her tongue out at me," Kim said.

Jody looked at them both and could do nothing but shake her head. "I'ma need the both of you to stop getting at each other like you are. Chloe, don't do it again."

Completely frustrated, Kim threw her hands up and decided to go back to her room.

"Kim, where are you going?" Jody asked.

"For real, Mom, that's all? Chloe is wearin' me out. I'm goin' to my room, Mom."

Jody wanted to hear about Kim's day, and she knew something was not right with her.

"Sit down and talk to me for a minute," she said. "What's wrong with you."

Kim took a deep breath, shook her head and answered, "Nothing mom."

"No no wasn't asking," Jody said to Kim.

"Rhetorical," Chloe said trying to be funny.

"Okay, you know what?" Jody quickly said, "I've about had it with your mouth, too Chloe. Now, stop it."

"See," Kim interjected.

"Eww, I don't recall asking for your assistance, at all. I got this. You know what—"

Jody had it with Kim and Chloe. Remember what Kim said about her mother at the park?

"Both of you are wearin' me out, and what is your problem?" she pointed at Kim and said.

"She plays too much, Mom. You never say anything to her, and if you do, all you say is stop," Kim yelled.

Jody looked at Kim and swung because Kim had completely lost her mind.

Kim moved so quick; she almost fell on the floor. She could not jump back quick enough. "Mommy."

"Bob—and—weave Kim," Chloe said cracking up.

"Oh lawd, that mouth and that tone almost sent you to be with Jesus. Now— Jody stood up—you don't worry about how Irun this household, all right. You just make sure you're not at the other end of it all. Now chill out."

A very frustrated Jody decided to step out the room to get herself together.

"You two stay here, do not move, and do not say a word to each other," she said and walked into the kitchen.

Once she completed her five-minute adult time out, she went back into the living room and noticed the blank looks on Kim's and Chloe's faces.

"You do your homework," she said pointing at Chloe, "and you come in the kitchen, right now."

"Mom, why do you want to talk so bad?" Kim asked Jody as calmly as she could.

"I don't understand why you're trying so desperately to avoid speaking to me. Let me start off by saying, I'm going to pretend that you did not just raise your voice at me, and your sister is younger than you, *seriously*," as if Kim lost her mind, "but yet you keep arguing with her. Did something happen at school today I should know about?"

"No, Mom," Kim said. "It was another day at school."

"Just another day at school," Jody said sarcastically.

"School was fine, Mom. I'm fine. Everything's fine."

Sending the message that she didn't want to talk; Kim leaned back against the wall and crossed her arms. Jody would not let it go because she knew Kim was not telling the truth. She asked again if something took place at school.

"I simply need to know what is going on with my child. Now, we can stay in this kitchen all night long or you can tell me what's on your mind?" Jody said.

"All right, here we go." Kim decided to have a seat because she knew this was not going to be an easy one. "I know someone who did something, that to me wasn't really smart," Kim said with much hesitation.

Jody interrupted, "Let me stop you right there, Kim. It sounds as though you are judging this person. Let's not forget, everyone does things that aren't cool with God or their parent. Secondly," she put her hand up to stop Kim before she said one word, "you are totally ticked off with this person.

Either way, it's not all right. Check your attitude before you tell me this story and get to the point. Please and thank you. Never mind the fact that you are not perfect either." Jody said.

"Putting it mildly, she's been acting really strange lately," Kim said. "Mom, I just don't want her to get into any trouble."

"Kim, what's going on?" She said very slowly. "I want to hear what you have to say, but my goodness," she stressed, "spill it, okay 'cause I'm forty, and God is still working with me on this patience thing, now. Quit trippin'."

Chloe walked in the room, and Kim realized she needed to apologize to her for earlier. She knew that her attitude was not right, and she could have handled the situation differently.

"Excuse me," Chloe said.

"I'm sorry, Chloe, about earlier," Kim said to Chloe.

"Mm-hm, okay." Chloe did not care to hear Kim's apology, and it showed.

Surprised at Chloe's response, Jody said, "Chloe, that's not nice! Your sister is trying to apologize to you. Turn around and look at her."

Chloe did not think she said anything wrong to Kim. But from the look on Jody's face, clearly, she did.

"I'm sorry, too?" Chloe looked at Kim, then turned to look at Jody, shrugged her shoulders and said. "I don't know what for, but..." She turned around and headed out the door.

"Chloe," Jody yelled, "what do you need?"

"Never mind," Chloe shouted from the living room, "goin' outside."

"All right do not go far and make sure you take your cell phone. She better have that phone with her. Sometimes I wonder if God is punishing me."

Kim looked at her mom, shook her head and thought to herself, *wait what is that supposed to mean*?

Jody turned to Kim and asked, "Who are you talking about, Kim?"

"I'm worried about Tonya, Mom."

Jody told Kim that no matter what we do or how far Tonya may stray away, God has not forgotten about her. Jody also, made Kim aware that we are to represent God and our parents well, and that cutting classes is not honoring God.

"Let me start by saying this," Jody stressed with a troubled look on her face, "I'm not having that out of you. You better not allow the issues of your friends to influence you to do something stupid like that.

I don't care about what everybody else's kids do. Ain't no birds gonna be flockin' nowhere together. You go to class from bell to bell. Do you hear me? I'm so serious right now. If you ever cut class or leave school, I would hurt you."

Kim interrupted Jody by saying, "Mom, I don't do that." She thought to herself, *wait how did mom know that*? "I don't cut class. I'm so *serious* when I say that I don't want to die."

"Yeah, you might as well call Children's Services right now," Jody answered back. "But what would make Tonya leave school like that, Kim? Do you know if she has done this before?" With eyebrows raised, Jody asked, "Do you think she may have left with a boy, maybe?" Jody gave Kim a look as to suggest something else.

Kim smiled and said, "Maybe, I don't know. I feel like this may lead to something else."

With a look of curiosity, Jody asked Kim, "Are you interested in any boys? 'Cause you know you need to ask me first."

"Trust me, Mom, when I am, you'll be the first to know. Can we talk about Tonya? How is it that this conversation keeps jumping to me? I'm good. You don't have to worry about me."

"Thank you, Jesus!" Jody stood up in the middle of the kitchen and began to praise God because she was reassured at that very moment, Kim was not having sex.

"All right I'm back. I'm just checking," Jody said. So, who is this boy she may have left school with? Do I need to beat someone down?"

Kim said, as she shook her head, "Mom, we don't beat up people anymore! Remember we're Christians."

"Oh yeah, that would be an issue. You know, the appearance of evil thing. I'm just playing. I'm serious, but I'm playing, though. I may be a Christian, but I'm not going to allow the enemy to hurt someone I care about."

"Yeah, okay, Mom. You can't blame the devil for beating someone up."

"Look Kim, what I need you to do is pray for Tonya and stop being so mad about things that are out of your control. Better yet, that has nothing to do with you. All you need to do is pray, you hear me. Not asking you, telling you."

"All right, Mom, I'll be in my room. You're the one that needs prayer," she added under her breath. "Man, I said she was crazy, Lord help us all."

"What was that?"

"Nothing, Mommy," Kim yelled. "I love you, gotta start my homework. We'll finish our conversation later," Kim said as she ran upstairs. "Man, that ended pretty good."

"Are you hungry, do you want some ice cream?" Jody yelled.

"No mom, how can you eat right now? And ice cream is not food." Kim shouted.

"'Cause I want some ice cream. What you mean? If you have a taste for ice cream, you get some ice cream. What, I'm just supposed to stop eating 'cause Tonya's acting up? I can pray while I eat."

Not hearing from Tonya made Kim concerned. God would take care of Tonya, and Kim was well aware of that fact; however, she was still concerned. Trying to distract herself, Kim turned on her radio and began to pick her outfit for the church service that night. While Kim was in her room, Jody and Chloe were in the kitchen preparing dinner before they had to leave. The hours were quickly going by, and Jody felt pressured to complete her work, finish dinner, and prepare for the worship service. Even though she was pressed for time, she could not allow that to interfere with her time with Chloe. The phone rang and Jody turned to tell Chloe to answer it, but she was no longer in the kitchen with her.

"I thought she was supposed to be helping me cook?" Jody said to herself. "That little thang done left the kitchen. Now I got to answer the phone too. Hello," Jody said.

"Hey Jody, this is Mrs. Karns. How are you?"

"I'm well and you?" Jody asked.

"I've certainly had better days," Mrs. Karns said as she exhaled.

"Was it a rough day at school today?" Jody asked with much concern.

"Well, you can say that. This has been one of those days I wish I could do all over again. You know rewind the clock?"

"Wow, I'm really sorry to hear that," Jody said. "I know what you mean though. I feel like I live in a house with crazy people," she said as she laughed. "I wish I could rewind some things, too. For example, when Kim first came home, she was acting all kinds of crazy . . ." Looking at the clock, Jody said, "Are you coming to church tonight? Maybe we can talk then."

"I'm going to try. I may be bringing some people with me. At least, I am hoping I will be. Well, I was calling to talk about a situation that may have taken place with some students from school."

"Let me guess, Tonya is one of those students? This has to be related to the story Kim was telling me when she got home."

"Yes, it is concerning Tonya," Mrs. Karns said with much dismay. "Do you know if she has talked to Kim this evening?"

"No, not that I'm aware of. Kim was acting pretty strange when she got home today from school. I'm a little concerned now. What is this about? Does this have something to do with Kim?"

"No, it doesn't. Tonya's parents have you listed as an emergency contact. I cannot get ahold of them, and no one has been able to reach them today at all. This isthe reason for my call. If you don't mind me asking, what did Kim tell you?"

"She was just telling me Tonya was hanging out with the wrong people. She's very worried about her. Tonya cut school and, to her knowledge, did not come back."

"We believe Tonya did leave school sometime between Study Hall and her lunch period with a couple of students. There was a shooting at the mall earlier today. I've talked to Principal Thompson, and everything is speculation at this point.

We are concerned because students do leave and hang out at the mall during school hours. We checked the attendance rosters, and they were among the students who were unaccounted for. We've been very busy this evening. Needless to say, some of us teachers and staff have been doing a lot of praying. I'm waiting to hear if it was in fact them."

"All right, depending on the time, I will be here or the church. You have to let me know. My God, is this really happening? Why is this happening? Regardless whose kids they are, this has to stop."

"From your mouth to God's ears, Jody," Mrs. Karns said as her voice quivered. "You'll get a call from Principal Thompson or me. Could I possibly speak with Kim?"

"Sure, one moment. I'll get her for you."

Jody walked upstairs to let Kim know the phone was for her. "Kim, telephone, it's Mrs. Karns."

"Okay—Hello," Kim said.

"Hello, Kim. How are you?" Mrs. Karns answered in a soft tone.

With less excitement, as she hoped it would be Tonya on the other end. "Hi, Mrs. Karns. I'm good, and you?"

"I'm well, thank you. Do you have a minute? I would like to speak with you about Tonya."

"Yeah, I'm just trying to find something to wear tonight. I can't wait. I think it is going to be a good service, and I have no clue what I'm going to wear."

Mrs. Karns giggled and asked, "Have you talked to Tonya?"

Kim began to feel anxious in her stomach. Not sure of what she was about to be told, her heart started beating very fast. *Why would Mrs. Karns be calling asking about Tonya, very strange*, Kim thought to herself.

"No, I haven't yet. I'm going to call her a little later. Why are you asking about Tonya? Did something happen?"

"Well, there was a situation at the mall today and—"

"Kim!" Jody yelled from the bottom of the steps.

"Mrs. Karns, one minute my mom is calling me."

Kim put the phone down to open the door. "Yes, Mom!" she yelled.

Jody ran up the stairs as she was telling Kim to turn on her television. Kim picked up the remote to turn it on. Remembering Mrs. Karns' concern about Tonya, and something about the mall, she started to panic.

Kim picked up the phone and asked, "Mrs. Karns, what is going on?"

"It's coming on right now, Kim. Turn to channel 10," Jody said.

"Okay, hold on one minute," Kim said. "Mom come here, hurry. Mom, what's this all about?"

Jody was just as concerned as Kim. Not knowing the answer, herself, she responded, "I'm not sure, Kim. Here it is."

"At approximately 1:00 p.m. today, a shooting took place a couple feet away from where I am standing. You see the police cars behind me? That is where the shooting actually happened. Police are not sure as of yet what led up to this shooting. They can tell us that there were at least four people involved, and I was also told that drugs might have been the center of this incident. At this time, they have no other information.

They are asking that if anyone is aware of this shooting and might have any information that will help, please contact your local police department. My name is Lisa Taylor, Cross Action News."

Kim fell to her knees and cried. "Why did you guys want me to watch this?" she screamed. "Is this a joke? Was Tonya there? I don't understand. How could this happen? Mrs. Karns?" She turned to look at her mom, "Mom, what is going on?"

It took everything for Mrs. Karns to hold back tears. Unsure of what to tell Kim, she simply said, "Kim, everything is going to be okay. We are not even certain Tonya was there. We only know she left school. We just need to pray that she is covered.

We have not heard from her, and we are quick to assume that this is about her. We do not have any information as of yet. We need to pray and trust God. If she was there, we need to trust that God covered her and everyone else involved. You know, Kim, we give the devil too much credit. Remember what we talked about earlier today. God will have the victory in the end. Now, I must get off the phone. I'm waiting for Principal Thompson to call me back."

"Mrs. Karns, if you find out anything, please let me know?" Kim asked. "Thank you for calling me and letting me know what's going on. I haven't heard from her at all, if I do, I will let you know."

"I will contact your mom as soon as I hear something."

"Did Mrs. Karns have any more information?" Jody asked.

"She didn't say anything else. Just that she will talk to you at church. Mom, I'm going to lie down for a little while. Please letme know if you hear anything."

"I will, baby girl," Jody said as she walked out of Kim's room.

Jody went down to the living room and began to pray. From her room, Kim could hear Jody praying. Kim dropped to her knees and threw her hands in the air. Tears began to flow down her face as she prayed with her mother. Jody in one room, Kim in the other, yet in tuned to the Holy Spirit. They called on Jesus.

"Oh, Lord, show Yourself strong. We call on You, Lord, right now, to move in a mighty and miraculous way.

We ask for favor on behalf of these people who were in the wrong place at the wrong time and for the ones who made the very bad choice to carry a gun. Lord, we know that our actions have consequences, but we pray for leniency, in Jesus's name. Mercy, Lord, have mercy on them, in Jesus's name. Father God, we know that You will get the victory when it's all said and done, and devil, you will not win! We come against any and everything that has a hold on theselives. We bind the devil in Jesus name, and pray that whatever he is planning will be brought to an end in Jesus Christ's holy name."

CHAPTER SUMMARY

I believe friendships are important to God. To be a good friend to someone is to love as God loves. A good friend holds the other accountable, gives sound advice, protects, and has the desire to see one another grow and succeed, in all aspects of life. There are incredible benefits to having great friends in our life, for emotional and spiritual support. Consider this scripture:

[9] "Two people are better off than one, for they can help each other succeed. [10] If one person falls, the other can reach out and help. But someone who falls alone is in real trouble. [11] Likewise, two people lying close together can keep each other warm. But how can one be warm alone? [12] A person standing alone can be attacked and defeated, but two can stand back-to-back and conquer. Three are even better, for a triple-braided cord is not easily broken."

Ecclesiastes 4:9-12 NLT

Another part of being a good friend is to know when to let go and allow your friend to learn and experience on their own. That does not mean completely backing off.

That does not mean you are not to care. Give that friend room to hear from God for him or herself. The Bible says that we must be patient with everyone and in every situation. Never forget that everyone's growth in the Lord is different. Pray and wait on God.

Things will happen that are out of our control, that is a given. We cannot always do everything in our own strength. But in every situation, we must pray, seek The Lord, and wait. We must begin to soak in the presence of God and wait for a response. Yes, *wait patiently* for the Lord. It can be hard to do, but if we want to make the right choice it must be done.

We must also remember; we are not only the reflection of our parents; we are the reflection of God as well. In our schools, in the workplace, in the streets, we are to model after Christ. You can run but you cannot hide. Remember, some may not know, however God does. He knows all and He sees *every single thing* you do. He knows what you are thinking, He knows your heart. Saying out of your mouth that you love The Lord, is not enough. Saying out of your mouth that you are a Believer, is just not enough.

People must see by the way we live, *Believer*, this is for us, just how much we love The Lord. The way we respond to certain situations, is not okay. Not only do people see you, but God does as well. We must do better. A scripture to consider:

"Delightfully loved ones, don't imitate what is evil, but imitate that which is good. Whoever does good is of God; whoever does evil has not seen God."
3 John 1:11 TPT

We must not be afraid to let go of the control and allow God to do what He says in the scripture. Never forget that we do not have to worry nor be discouraged because He is on the scene and will work it out. God will give us the strength to walk through whatever storm or test we may face at any given moment. He is very good at juggling our issues and the issues of the world, love us, carry us, protect us, and so much more and all at the same time. He's got skills like that—one piece of evidence of that skill is the creation of the world, and that is only one.

CHAPTER TWELVE

Tim was otherwise preoccupied and never returned with Nika's money or her product. The longer Nika sat at home and did nothing, the more furious she became. She began to call around to some of the people she knew he ran with to see where he could be. The more calls she made, the hotter her anger grew. Three hours later, she found out Tim may have been with Leah. Everyone knew they ran together. Nika drove around the neighborhood, looking for Leah and with every intention of doing whatever she needed to do to get information out of her. Unsuccessful in locating Leah, Nika asked someone where she might be.

Nika saw one of her boys on the corner by the carryout. Deciding to stop and ask, she pulled over. "Have you seen Leah?"

Intimidated by her, he blurted out anything to get her moving. "No, but I know she hangs with that girl Tonya. She may be with her."

"Who is Tonya and where can I find her, since if I find her, I'll find Leah? I hope you don't think I don't know what ya doin', my man. Get on with it, and if I'm not satisfied with what I find, I'll come find you."

Nika is one of those drug dealers who thinks she runs the town, and everyone around her feels the same way.

"Well, I don't know where Tonya live, but she goes to that big church on the corner. She may be there. There are mad cars in the lot. Somethin' is goin' on," he said.

"You talkin' 'bout the one right there on the corner of Smith and Watkins?" Nika asked him.

"Yeah man that's the one. That's where all the high school students go, really," he said.

Nika rolled up her window and drove off and made her way to the church. Not a happy individual, she pulled up right in front of the building, stopped the car, grabbed her gun from under the driver's seat, and stepped out of the car. Looking around to make sure she was not being watched, she lifted her jacket, put her gun behind her back, and shut the door. She walked up to the door of the church, and with no hesitation, she opened the door and walked in.

"Hello there and welcome," the usher said to Nika. "Any particular place you would like to sit?"

Nika looked at the usher with a smirk, laughed and said, "No need to sit anywhere. I ain't stayin'."

"You're not staying for the service?" he asked with a puzzled look on his face.

"Nah, I'm not staying," she replied.

"Is there a reason why you're not interested in staying?" the usher asked. "You are certainly in the right place."

"I mean no disrespect, but I'm just here looking for someone. That's it that's all," Nika said to get him to stop talking.

"I see, and that someone might be who?" the usher asked. "Maybe I can help you find him or her."

"This person is a she, and I was told she would be here tonight. Trust me, that is the only reason I'm here," she tried to say calmly. "Anything outside of that you can really keep though."

In all sincerity, the usher said, "Well, I'm not sure if you would be able to find her right now. There's a lot going on. But if you would like to take a seat, I would be happy to try. Does this someone have a name?" he asked.

"Her name is Tonya. Really, I am looking for Leah, but I was told she might be here with Tonya."

"Tonya," the usher said to himself. "I think I know who that is. She's a friend of Kim's, right?"

"I guess. I don't know who Kim is," Nika said.

"All right then, let me sit you down, and I can try and find either of them for you," he stated.

"Hold on one moment, please, and thank you, 'cause I'm not trying to get caught up. What's goin' on tonight?"

The atmosphere Nika was in was very overwhelming for her.

"We have a guest speaker here tonight. But with the way service has been going so far, he may not get a chance to speak," the usher answered.

"Why you say that? You know what, never mind," Nika said, "and the cross?" She nodded.

"Pastor just had it brought out a little bit ago," he said. "Do you know what the cross represents?"

Something I have had an issue with, even though I know it is always a choice, Nika thought to herself.

She became very offended and reacted, "Come on man, I might be thugged out, but I know Jesus. That's my dude. I just don't come here."

"Are you sure you don't want to take a seat?" the usher asked. "I mean, I'm used to standing here, but if you want to keep me company, you're more than welcome," he said and laughed.

Nika did not get the humor.

"Are there any prayer requests you may have tonight?" he asked.

"Yo, you can save that, too," she said with a smirk. "We both know you will not pray for someone like me," Nika mumbled. "Christians are funny to me. You say you'll pray, but you probably won't."

"It's my job to pray for everyone, even people I don't know. Here you go, everyone is writing their prayer requests on these cards. We're all going to pray over them tonight. Is there anything that you need God to do for you? If there is, you can write it on this card. Here, take this pen and write your prayer request at your seat. Right this way, please."

"Fine," Nika said and took the card. "But I'm good in the back."

"Right this way, please." He motioned for Nika to follow him. He got to the middle and continued toward the front and, of course, Nika was not feeling that at all.

"No, no, excuse me. Psst. Psst," Nika said trying her best to get his attention."Not so close to the front, man. I don't wanna."

Where he stopped Nika definitely did not want to go. Although the usher did not hear her say differently, he had his reasons for wanting her on the second row.

Before Nika walked in the building, her mission was to hurt someone at first chance. The usher took Nika to her seat. The Praise Team began singing a song "All I Need," which set the atmosphere. Remember everything happens for a reason.

The longer she stayed, the more fidgety she became. As the service went on, after the singing and the dancing, the anointing was so strong that Nika began to loosen up. The pastor stood up and talked about everything that had taken place, so everyone would know, the band and Praise Team followed right behind. Nika sat wiping away tears, too intense for her. She twisted and turned in her seat. It was hard for her to believe she was and back in church after so long, no matter what the reason.

"We want to thank everyone for coming out this evening. I believe that God is going to continue to speak to us. He has prepared our hearts and will minister to us in every way possible if we continue to allow Him to. He is able to reach us by His divine purpose, will, and plan. We may or may not understand, nevertheless, He will continue to speak as long as we continue to listen. Amen?"

Nika sat in her seat perfectly still, unable to take her eyes off the pastor of the church.

"In His conversation with us tonight, I pray that you all have received a blessing and that God will meet the needs of His people right where you are. We have been praying for this service for some time, that God will move on the lives of everyone here tonight. Know that you are not here by chance. God knew who would be here tonight, and He has a message, a free gift. It is not about Christmas. It is not about what you can do well or not do well. It is for everyone here, just because of who you are. God has seen your life and pulled you into this place at this very hour so that you would be entangled, forever intertwined with and by His love, His mercy, and His grace."

The pastor introduced the guest speaker, and this is where it all began. Nika was experiencing things she had never felt before. Embarrassed to get up and leave, yet uncomfortable where she was. Although she knows the Lord, she has never had a notion of divine appointment.

Where is Tim? I can't believe I got myself in this situation, Nika thought to herself. I came here to look for someone, not sit in a church service. I feel weird, but I can't just get up and leave 'cause he just had to put me right in the front. Why did I come here? Now this guest speaker is about to get up. I'm really going to be here all night, Nika thought to herself.

"Good evening, body of Christ. It is good to be in the house of the Lord tonight."

He picked up his Bible, grabbed his iPad, and moved them off to the side.

Yep, we're gonna be here all night. I'll figure out the right time to slip out. Soon as they take up an offering, I'm out, Nika thought.

"Let me just get right to the point," he said, "There is someone here who has turned their back on God, and you're feeling some kinda way about that." He stood in one spot motionless, speaking clearly through the microphone.

"One day needing to be a light in a dark place and the next day being influenced by darkness. Pressured   into being accepted, feeling the guilt you feel because of who your friends are. Our teens are hurting, and some parents don't even know it. This pressure I am talking about has you at every moment of every single day, wanting to do the right thing, but can't because you're torn between doing the right thing, and survival, or doing the right things, and acting out of your emotions, your flesh, if you will. You try to be a man, a woman, but not having the right model of how a man or a woman is supposed to be makes it pretty difficult. At the same time, you do your best to be the man of the family, but with no demonstration on how to pull that off.

There is someone in this room tonight victimized by their culture. They continually surround themselves with the wrong people to get money, and not caring about the consequences in the long run. This is the pressure that our young generation face. If you need a title for tonight's message, it would be "I Choose." You see, we are the sum of the decisions, or choices if you will, we will make in our lives. We, one day, will have to give an answer for all the choices we have made," he said.

He walked down the steps in Nika's direction, and she shifted in her seat.

"Please, do not come over here and say anything to me. I don't need that type of attention," Nika said to herself.

"It's hard sometimes to be the voice of God," the minister said, "to know and say the right things, give the right advice, and it is not adhered to or just looked over. You have to question, am I doing the right thing? Saying the right thing? Asking the right questions? Why am I doing what I do, and should I keep on doing it? Is there anyone in here lost and being led by the devil every single day? You're making your way harder, trying to be something you're not. There are a lot of people in the church that are that way. We must choose to be an influence and not be influenced by the things of this world. Today is the day to choose which way you want to live and whom you will serve. Aren't you tired of running, tired of hitting your head against the wall? Day in and day out, going through the same trials and finding no solutions. If you're not living this way, then you know someone who is.

Who in here is on the fence, torn between two opinions or perceptions, judging what you have seen and what you think you know to be true? We must realize that what we think we know is not always the truth. Have you had enough church, just enough to make you sick?

There are many people who have. They hear and assume things, and it keeps them out of the church where they know they need to be. You may have witnessed situations in the church that were wrong or out of place. You probably have seen people who call themselves Believer and live the life of a sinner. But we must choose not to pass judgment, for there is no perfect person or Christian.

Does everyone here understand that you cannot live your life through someone else? You cannot possibly know God for who He is through the eyes of someone else. You must choose to let go of the life that you are living because it is not of God," the minister said.

Nika stood up, and the minister looked over at her and once again paused, showing no emotion, he walked in the other direction. Saying nothing, he lifted his eyes to the ceiling.

"Yes Lord," he said. "You must be willing to let go of the lifestyle you are living and allow God to love you. You know that the things you are doing are wrong and the voice that you are hearing inside from time to time is the voice of the Lord. It tells you, you must choose to be all in. 'You gave Me your attention at one point. I was your first love, now I am your second, your third,' says God," he continued to speak. All the while his back is toward Nika. She stood there paralyzed, unable to move.

"You must choose to listen to the voice inside of you because it is the voice of the Lord, and He loves you enough to not let you go. Trust me when I tell you, choose now before it is too late. For the life that you are living does not guarantee life tomorrow," he said.

"'Put those things down that are keeping you from truly knowing Me and My love,'" says God. 'Walk away from the things of this world that keep you from traveling down a straight path, which is the path that leads to Me. Yes, the road gets rocky, but that is why I sent you a comforter to speak to you in those hard times,'" says God, 'to help you make the right decisions.'

You must have a willing heart to be emptied out in order to be filled with the spirit of the living God," the minister said. "You must be willing to give God a chance to show you a better way to live."

Nika sat back down in her seat and continued to cry. "I know he is talking to me. That is me. Okay, what do I do now? How do I do this? I've done so much dirt and hurt a lot of people. Why would He want to? Why would He want to?" Nika asked herself.

"You never have to question whether God loves you. You never have to question whether He has chosen you. 'I have not forgotten you,'" says God. "There are people who are attempting to be the voice of reason for someone else. You do your best to be a friend, an intercessor, trying to hold up the arms and the life of a friend, all the while not feeling appreciated and wondering if you can do it. Do you continue trying to fix things? Asking yourself, do they understand your intentions and that they are pure? When are you going to pray and wait to hear from God before allowing yourself to get angry and overreact? What kind of example are you setting for the people around you? Is it the life of a Christian or the life of a sinner? Which do you choose?

Each of you was given a card and a pencil when you came in this evening. Take this time to write down everything you need, want, or desire God to do in your life. If you need to be emptied out so that God can fill you with the things you need to survive, write those things down. Write down your prayer requests and the intercessors will pray over them. They will pray while you pray. We will stand in the gap for you, stand with you, cry with you, and praise with you. If you want to just come up for prayer, you can do that as well. After you are done writing, come up and lay it down at the cross. Now the key is, when you lay it down, you leave it here at the cross. You must walk away and not look back. Do not take it back by talking about it, worrying about it, or thinking about it. When you are ready to release your grip on those things, walk away."

After a while Nika stood up again, took a deep breath, and put her hand behind her back. A few feet away from Nika was the usher she talked to at the door.

"You cannot stand with the devil and stand with God at the same time," the minister said.

The usher motioned to another usher, moving his finger from his right eye and held up three fingers, signaling him to keep an eye on Nika and move on three.

The minister noticed what Nika was doing out of the corner of his eye and said, "Come boldly before the throne of God."

Nika began to pull the gun from her back, the ushers ran toward her, ready to take her down, and the minister stopped them. She started walking toward the cross, raised her hand toward heaven, laid her gun down, and the church went up in an uproar. People began to run, jump, and shout. They cried, danced, and sang.

"There is nothing you can do that will keep God from loving you. You must understand that God is love."

16 "We know how much God loves us, and we have put our trust in his love. God is love, and all who live in love live in God, and God lives in them."

1 John 4:16 NLT

"Do you know how much God loves you?" he turned to ask Nika. "You can forever put your trust in Him. Believe that no matter what you do, He will always love you. He's been waiting on you, young lady."

Nika, the biggest drug dealer in the city, lay down on the floor and began to cry.

"I'm sorry," she cried out.

She gave her life back to the Lord that night. Being willing to lay down her devilish lifestyle for the Lord was the best decision she had ever made. Let there be another...

Remember the prayer of salvation in the chapter summary after chapter 10. It does not stop there. Get plugged in to a church so you can be among a great body of believers. There they can help you along your new journey, your new life in Him.

CHAPTER SUMMARY

[7] "The end of the world is coming soon. Therefore, be earnest and disciplined in your prayers. [8] Most important of all, continue to show deep love for each other, for love covers a multitude of sins."
1 Peter 4:7–8 NLT

God wants each and every one of us to be ready for when His Son, Jesus The Christ, returns. We must be serious about getting to know Him, our walk with Him, and our relationship with Him, and in our prayer lives. It is very important that we love one another, look out for one another, and share God's love with one another. We must be open to change, willing to be emptied out, and ready to receive all God has for us.

Each and every one of us is given the choice to live for God or the devil. There are many of us who straddle the fence and that is no longer acceptable to God. We know what to do, and we do not do it. We love the Lord with all our heart and soul. However, we choose to do things that are not pleasing in His sight.

¹⁵ "I know all the things you do, that you are neither hot nor cold. I wish that you were one or the other! ¹⁶ But since you are like lukewarm water, neither hot nor cold, I will spit you out of my mouth!"

Revelation 3:15–16 NLT

Do you want to be spit out? A wise woman once told me, "Stop it, and get it together." Simply stop allowing the devil to use, guide, and direct you. Either we are for God or against Him. We must choose, stop running, and stop trying to hide. Understand this, we cannot hide from God. He is omnipresent. Wherever you are, trust me, He is there also. He knows everything about us. He knows us better than we know ourselves.

⁵ "I knew you before I formed you in your mother's womb. Before you were born I set you apart and appointed you as my prophet to the nations."

Jeremiah 1:5 NLT

CHAPTER THIRTEEN

Paul sat in front of a group of teenagers who were wounded and broken. Scars so deep, it has taken a lot of prayer and time for them to heal. A Few come from broken homes and receive more love in the streets. With shattered hearts they long to be receive love from their parents or at least care about what happens to them. Some with single-parent mothers, single-parent fathers, trying their best to raise their children alone. Two-parent households, yet one is left doing everything with little to no help. It is hard for them, and the children do not understand. Some, whose parents work more than one job and still struggle daily. Their teens sell drugs because they think it would help make ends meet. The children end up on the streets, in jail, or worse because they are wounded. This simply guides them to a stream of bad choices.

No longer can they hide. They have been arrested. Paul and Kim are going to do whatever they can to change the path the teens are taking.

"What are some things that are really hard for you to handle?" Paul asked.

Joey, one of the teens attending the group, said, "I am dealing with too many people in my business. I can't go anywhere or do anything without my parents being on my case."

"All right, everybody has to agree that everything we talk about will remain within this group. Do we all agree?" Paul asked.

All of the teens, including Paul and Kim, agreed to not share what takes place at their youth group with anyone, and Kim began to talk directly to Joey. "Do you mind?" Kim turned to ask Paul, and he gave her the floor. "Joey be completely honest, okay," Kim said. "Is there, by chance, any reason why your parents shouldn't question you about where you're going, what you're doing at any given time? You've given them no reason to question?"

Joey looked at Kim, then to Paul, ashamed to say anything. Tricia, Joey's friend, spoke up and said, "It stays here, right, and no judgment?"

"Yes," Kim and Paul said at the same time.

"I can't say that I am the greatest son in the world, but I try. My parents aren't even around enough to care what I do. That's why I don't understand why they care now," Joey said.

"I hate that I have to deal with this mess. Granted I'm seventeen and graduate in a year, but they don't care about that. I may make bad choices sometimes, but I'm graduating soon. Does that matter? No, it doesn't. I have questions about colleges, relationships, stress, and they are nowhere around. So, I go hang out at Tricia's. Sure, I've gotten into trouble and that has nothing to do with her, but they think she's a bad influence on me."

"Yeah," Tricia said, "and I have no problem goin' through whatever for my boy."

"Um, are you guys—" Kim began to ask them a question and was interrupted.

"No, we're not," Tricia cut in and said. "We're friends and always have been, since the first grade. This is our last year of high school, man. That's a big deal, I think, no matter what our parents or the government says."

"Joey," Paul said, "you have to understand that parents too have many things they deal with. Outside of you and everything they have to deal with, things can be stressful. No excuse, I know, but try to understand. Trust me when I tell you, it hurts, yes, but give them time. You pray about everything you are going through and ask God to work it out for you."

Paul picked up his Bible and began to read, "*Honor your father and your mother, as the Lord your God has commanded you, so that you may live long and that it may go well with you in the land the Lord your God is giving you. Deuteronomy 5:16.*"

"I get that, and I need a lot of work in that area," Joey said.

"Your days will be long on the earth," Kim said to the group. "Life is confusing and sometimes messy. We are not going to always know exactly what to do. We cannot fault our parents, try to understand and trust that the Lord will make it all right."

Paul looked over at Kim and nodded at her to share with them about her home life.

"It's just my mother, my sister Chloe, and me at home. My mother is a single parent, and she tries very hard to make ends meet and I know that. Mom does not know that I am aware of her tears. I know she stays up after Chloe and I go to bed, crying herself to sleep. I know that she works extra hours to make certain we have what we want and need," Kim expressed.

"It's not by chance that I am talking to you specifically, Joey," she stressed. "God has a plan for you. He is going to use you to reach your parents. I don't know what they are facing right now, but He says to not fear because He is in control. Let them see the God in you and that will draw them to the Lord. God has a job for you to do, and He's giving you the choice to obey."

"Amen," Paul said. "Our last topic for the night is how many of you are dealing with drug, alcohol, or sex issues?"

A touchy subject for some to talk about, however, Paul had no fear. All of the teens sat and looked at each other, no one wanting to answer Paul's question. Paul and Kim didn't want any of them to be afraid to share what they're going through, as the group is to be a safe haven for them, a place for where they can be unashamed to speak their truth.

"You cannot be touched by God and remain the same," Paul said. "He will begin to change some things in your life and disrupt sin. You must also understand that your change, your transition to change, will not happen overnight. You have to allow that change to take place in your life. You don't have to know what it is. You just have to trust that God is in control and He knows what He's doing, ask Him."

Paul is the perfect youth leader for this group of teens. His passion goes beyond what he can explain. You can see it in the way he interacts with them. The more time Kim spends with him, the more she likes what she sees.

"You must trust that you are strong enough to withstand whatever"—Kim knows that firsthand—"and you must know that on the other side of that thing you will come out victorious. You have to choose to make whatever change necessary in your life. Start with the crowd you run with, then with your way of thinking and the way you talk. You must let go of the control and let the love of the Lord into your heart, fully. You don't have time to mess around anymore, guys.

Don't you get it? Everlasting life is not promised if you continue to do the things you do. I'ma need all of you to get it together, once and for all," Kim said and laughed. Really, guys, God loves us, and He knows it's hard and that is why we have His grace."

The hour had gotten late. Paul and Kim needed to get the teens fed and straighten the room. Before doing so, Paul wanted the group to pray for one another. As he counted them into four, Kim began to pray.

"Who is ready to be committed? I mean totally open to the Lord," she said, "now is the time for each and every one of you to be all in, all of your problems, all of your questions, give them to the Lord, and leave them there. We need everyone in their groups of four. We want each of you to share within your group. Whatever that issue is whether big or small. Share and pray within your own group. Paul and I will close the prayer, and then we will eat and prepare to go home."

CHAPTER SUMMARY

The last teen had left for the night, Paul and Kim had to stay later to clean and lock up. Paul took advantage of the time with no interruptions to talk to Kim. He felt she was the perfect person to help with the youth group part-time. He watched how Kim interacted with the teens and how she allowed the Lord to use her to speak into their lives, and he knew she would do well.

Paul's job is not to take the place of their parents, but to assist the Lord in meeting them where they are. Paul's passion is to help guide them through there are as of struggle and to pray for them whenever needed. Some are slipping farther away, and his concerns are for those teens who are lost and hurting and have nowhere to go and no one to talk to. What do they do when their backs are against the wall? Consistent in his approach and message to allow the Lord to empty out the blockage, Paul continues to pray. His prayer is for those things that are keeping the youth from receiving all He has for them.

Not all of our youth have positive-speaking people in their lives, a place to go and hear the Word, and receive love. Not all of our children have an outlet, such as sports, art, or music, to get them through or friends to encourage them. It should always be our mission as Christians, parents, and leaders to pray and help our youth. That saying, *it takes a village* is a true statement.

CHAPTER FOURTEEN

Kim opened the door to her room and said good night to her mom and Chloe. She kept thinking about the youth group, specifically Joey and Tricia. She sees so much of herself in both teens and wants so desperately to help them. After how she handled the situation with Tonya, Kim does not feel equipped to do anything, but that does not matter to God.

"It's been a very long night," Kim said and climbed into bed. "My pillow is calling me."

Kim saw the hall light go out underneath her door, she turned over and closed her eyes. No sooner did she put a good dent in the pillow, she heard a door shut and her phone ring. "Are you serious, who in the world? It's 1:00 a.m., dang it! You've got to be kidding me, Paul."

"Hey, Kim, just wanted to call and talk. I can't sleep."

"Well, I can with no problem, I might add," Kim said.

"I apologize. I was thinking about you and needed to see how you were," Paul said.

Paul tried his best not to completely give away the fact that he had feelings for her. Little did he know that after the evening they had with the meeting and then dinner, Kim was beginning to share the same feelings.

"Paul, what is goin' on, and why are you not asleep?"

"I can't sleep for some reason. I guess I'm still amped about the meeting tonight, among other things."

Curious Kim asked, "What other things are you referring to, Paul?"

"Well, now, I have a lot on my mind I would like to talk to you about," Paul said clearing his throat. "You know the meeting and . . ."

"And what, Paul? I don't mean to rush, I'm just sleepy," Kim said softly.

"Kim, I understand you're sleepy, but I really need to talk to you. Have you talked to Tonya yet?"

Paul decided to wait until it felt right to tell Kim why he really called her.

"I don't know why I haven't heard from her yet. She hasn't called me or texted me. I can't believe that either. That's my girl, but the more I think about it, the madder I get. I would hate to think that it had something to do with—never mind," Kim said. "I can't control the situation, and I'm not able to show her that she's loved by so many people. I know it's not my job to watch her but, at the same time, that's my friend. However, she's not trying to deal with me right now, and that's all right, too. I know now that I'm not in the position to help anybody" —her voice shook— "and you can't be friends with everybody."

Paul paced as he tried to find the right words to say to Kim. After a while, he mustered up the nerve to be straight with her. "Kim, you know that it is the same with friendships," he said.

"Okay, I guess so," she said.

"When people are in relationships with no growth, without each person being fulfilled, you tend to grow apart." Paul took a deep breath and said, "It's the same with friendships. You are growing, she is not. You are excelling, she is not. Your spiritual life is off the hook, and from what I can tell, hers is not. You can't continue to blame yourself. She is dang near an adult."

"I'm not blaming myself. Okay, not anymore. Tonya is my friend, Paul. I feel like I am growing spiritually, especially after tonight. My issues are growing, too. I do believe we are growing apart as friends. That's crazy, huh? We've been friends for so long."

"Did you get a chance to have a conversation with her?" Paul asked.

"I did. When I walked down to the three of them, she acted like I wasn't there."

"I know you didn't expect anything different, did you?"

"I certainly didn't expect to be ignored." Kim said. "It ticked me off, too. Then Jeff—you know Jeff, right? Anyway, he came up behind me and pushed me. That was her opportunity to sneak away. Oh no, but your girl asked me if I wanted to smoke their weed."

"Don't worry about them, Kim." Paul laughed and asked again if they had any conversation. Kim explained how they did talk, and it did not go well. "She ticked me off, I ticked her off and, man, I thought we would never talk again. However, we did, eventually. The kicker is she left school with Leah and Tim. It's not like her. I haven't talked to her since that last conversation," Kim said.

She went on to tell Paul about the shooting that took place. Praying that Tonya was not involved, they prayed that whoever it could have been that God has mercy on them. Paul could hear in Kim's voice she was hurting. He put on his shoes and grabbed his keys, talking to her the entire time and not letting on he was coming to her.

"Kim, put on your jacket and shoes please, and come outside." Paul sat in his car until he saw her come out on the balcony.

"Paul, I'm not—Did he just hang up on me?" Kim looked at the phone for a second and laid it down on the bed. While grabbing her jacket and shoes, she put her mini flashlight in her mouth. *It's dark as heck*, she thought to herself, *this dude is crazy, almost 2:00 a.m.* She shook her head and sat down on the bed to put on her shoes.

A few minutes went by, and Kim heard a tap on her French doors.

"What the mess?" she said in a loud whisper, trying not to wake up her mom and Chloe.

I guess Paul decided not to wait for Kim to come out onto the balcony, too funny.

"What are you doing?" she said.

"Well I . . . ." Paul said.

"Rhetorical. How long have you been standing there? You know that was a stalker move right there, for real. You better be glad I know you."

"What was you gonna do, Ms. Thang?" Paul said and laughed.

"Mini flashlight to the forehead, that's what. Hold on, I'll be out in two point two," she said. "Have a seat right there," she pointed her light in the right direction. "No hurting yourself allowed."

Kim walked out onto the deck and sat next to him. She pulled a blanket out of the warmer and sat back. "Now what brings you out here this hour of the night?"

"I wanted to check on my friend. That's why I'm out at this hour. Not to mention, what I have to say can't be said over the phone."

"What is it, Paul, that's so important?"

Kim was beginning to get antsy and wanted to know why. Paul looked at Kim and said nothing right away. He grabbed her hand, with his head down, he tried to get the nerve to come out and say it. Kim's heart began to beat faster with expectation as she waited. Paul did not want to confuse Kim or cause her to question him after he said what he needed to say.

No more hesitating, Paul moved his chair closer to face her, with one finger, he touched her chin. He looked into her eyes and said, "I'm in love with you and have been for some time now. I can't nor do I want to hide the way I feel anymore. It hurts too much. I think of you as more than a friend now. Come here, give me some sugar."

"No wait," Kim said and pushed him away. "What happened to Tonya being your *first lady*?"

"Really, Kim, did you really think that?"

Completely stunned, Kim never suspected Paul would ever feel this way about her. Waiting for the right moment to respond without crying, she looked at him as she frequently did. Tilting her head to the side and eyebrow raised, she leaned back and asked softly, "Why are you telling me this now, when you know I'm leaving? How do you know anyway?"

"Yes, I am sure, Kimberly, and there is no way I was going to let you leave here without knowing how I really feel about you. We have known each other for so long, Kim. This isn't coincidental. You know me," he said.

"God has allowed me to see you and for you to see me. I was not going to let another moment of another day go by without telling you how I felt about you, and I had to do it to your face. You gonna shoot me down, Kim? You know you care about me. You do care about me don't you, Kim?"

Your life and the things that take place
in it can never be a secret...

SCRIPTURES
THE PASSION TRANSLATION,
THE NEW KINGS JAMES
& THE NEW LIVING
TRANSLATION
AS THEY APPEAR IN THE BOOK

Chapter 1
John 15:12-13
2Corinthians 3:18-19

Chapter 2
James 4:17
Galatians 5:16-23

Chapter 3
Romans 6:11-14
Psalms 3:13-15
Romans 12:1-2
Romans 14:10

Chapter 4
Matthew 7:1-2

Chapter 5
James 1:19
1 Thessalonians 5:23

Chapter 6
1 John 5:21
Exodus 20:4-6
1 Corinthians 10:13-15

Chapter 7
1 King 19:12
John 14:27
John 1:9
Philippians 4:4-7
Psalms 34:1-8
1 Peter 5:7
Revelation 3:20

Chapter 8
Proverbs 3:5-8
Psalms 32:8
Matthew 6:33

FIRST EDITION SCRIPTURES NOT APPEARING IN THIS EDITION

---

1 Corinthians 10:13

"The temptations in your life are no different from what others experience. And God is faithful. He will not allow the temptation to be more than you can stand. When you are tempted, he will show you a way out so that you can endure."

Proverbs 19:21

"You can make many plans, but the Lord's purpose will prevail."

John 16:32–33

"A time in life is coming and in fact has come when you will be scattered, each to your own home. You will leave me all alone. Yet I am not alone, for my Father is with me. I have told you these things, so that in Me you may have peace. In this world you will have trouble. But take heart! I have overcome the world."

Matthew 11:28:

"Come to me, all of you who are weary an carry heavy burdens and I will give you rest."

Psalms 37:7

"Rest in the Lord and wait patiently for Him".

WRITE THE VISION
& MAKE IT PLAIN
HABAKKUK 2:2

NOTES

NOTES

NOTES

NOTES

NOTES

NOTES

NOTES

NOTES

NOTES

NOTES